# THE PERFECT LOAF

## Angus Dunn

TWO RAVENS
PRESS

Published by Two Ravens Press Ltd
Green Willow Croft
Rhiroy
Lochbroom
Ullapool
Ross-shire IV23 2SF

**www.tworavenspress.com**

The right of Angus Dunn to be identified as author of this work has been asserted by him in accordance with the Copyright, Designs and Patent Act, 1988.

ISBN: 978-1-906120-10-8

British Library Cataloguing in Publication Data. A CIP record for this book can be obtained from the British Library.

Designed and typeset in Sabon by Two Ravens Press.
Cover design by David Knowles and Sharon Blackie based on a photograph of the author by David Knowles.

Printed on Forest Stewardship Council-accredited paper by Biddles Ltd., King's Lynn, Norfolk.

**Mixed Sources**
Product group from well-managed forests, controlled sources and recycled wood or fiber
www.fsc.org  Cert no. TT-COC-002303
© 1996 Forest Stewardship Council
FSC

# About the Author

Angus Dunn is from the Highlands of Scotland and is the author of the novel *Writing in the Sand* (Luath Press, 2006) which was shortlisted for the 2007 Saltire Society Scottish First Book of the Year Award.

Angus was awarded the 1995 Robert Louis Stevenson Prize and the 2002 Neil Gunn Short Story prize. His short stories have been published in many literary magazines and in collections such as *New Writing Scotland* and *Macallan Shorts*. Stories have also been broadcast on Radio 4, Radio Scotland and Lochbroom FM.

His poetry has been published in many Scottish magazines and anthologies.

He was brought up in Aultbea and Cromarty, and now lives near Strathpeffer in Ross-shire.

*For more information about the author, see*
**www.tworavenspress.com**

# Acknowledgements

Some of the short stories in this collection have been published previously in magazines or anthologies. They are:

*A Hard Place (1992)*, *Many Legs (1994)* and *Reading the Signs (2004)* in New Writing Scotland, *Jamie's Teeth* in The Edinburgh Review, *Parts* in Chapman, *Carrying the Light* in Northwords, *Scrimshaw* and *Unravelling* in Macallan Shorts (Polygon, 2002). *The Perfect Loaf* was published in the West Highland Free Press and *Looking for the Spark* was published in the anthology 'Looking for the Spark' (Harper Collins, 1994, in association with the Scottish Arts Council).

*For A and J*

# Contents

# Boundaries

# Boundaries

There is the doorstep, and there is the butcher's knife. There is the promise of a book. And the elvers. These are the landmarks of this place.

First, there is the doorstep, where nothing ever happened, again and again, for year after year.

There was thyme growing on the edge of that step, growing slowly, an inch in a year. And everything that could be seen from that doorstep took part in the same easy flow of time.

I sit there in the sunshine and the rain. I sit there at five years old and at ten. The concrete of the step has always had that chipped edge and corner: and then one year, and always thereafter, it has always had the thyme covering those wounds.

From that step, the sounds of the house are audible. The new baby is crying as her nappy is changed. She is crawling on the step beside me. She is running on the grass, she is crying from a fall by the fuchsia bush as the wind whips her hair.

Down the hill is another marker of this domain. Behind the general stores, the butcher's shop. There is sawdust on the floor, renewed every morning, but always with bloody flecks in it, discarded fragments of fat.

There is always another customer in there, and always the butcher leans towards me as I go in. His hand reaches out and his knife flashes towards my crotch. 'Sausages! Sausages!' He beams his red meaty smile for the benefit of the other customer.

If there is no-one else in the shop, I do not go in. I wait, counting the lemonade bottles in the wooden crates.

In the house itself, there are countless eddies where time is locked. At the table, I read the labels of jam jars, the sides of cereal boxes. I know every word. A voice says, 'We really must get him some good books. He's old enough for ...' The titles of the half-promised books change, the pattern is constant. On the sideboard is a serpentine pattern of veneer that a finger can follow mindlessly, does follow mindlessly and endlessly, year after year. The pattern is always complete: later, the broken edges are the way it has always been. Twilight creeps through the house, as a voice says 'This is the BBC Home Service...'

The eels were a part of that small domain too, but almost accidentally. They pass through at their own time, from a secret part of their own world, through the edge of our world, then into another, hidden part of their own.

Whenever there is a storm in Spring, elvers come out of our cold-water tap. Someone says that there must be a crack in the pipe, and the elvers crawl into it. Someone says that eels can travel a hundred yards over wet ground. Someone tells the story about the six-foot conger Uncle Colin caught. Someone agrees that they always tangle your fishing line.

I always listen, waiting for the six-foot conger to punctuate the pattern.

After a storm, I go down to the stream. Below the bridge, smooth rocks protrude above the water. They are covered with elvers, slithering over the wet stone. There are so many coming upstream that the burn cannot hold them.

I sit there, watching the elvers moving over the stones and through the bridge. I cannot stop watching, although I almost wish to. I am in the domain still, but it is the very edge of the pattern.

# A Hard Place

# A Hard Place

After school we would play on the seaweedy beams under the pier. Neither of us could swim, but we never fell in. Or we would go to your house the long way, up and through the moors. Other times, we explored the old gun emplacements near the beach, each concrete shelter full of rusty barbed wire and water. In Spring, frogspawn covered the surface. Later you showed me how to cut the tails off the tadpoles, to help them turn into frogs. They couldn't swim when you dropped them back in the water.

◆◆◆

It was the summer holidays, I remember. We turned off the road at the Manse, down onto the round-stone beach. The shoreline curved back, and round the bend was the gravel quarry, where a well-thrown rock could dislodge large slabs of gravel cliff. Or was that later? Perhaps the hillside was still rough pasture then.

◆◆◆

On Saturday mornings I was happy to dawdle through the crofts to your house. You were always in bed. While I waited, your mother gave me tea and toast, as if I was another adult in her house. The tea was sweet, the toast thick with butter. Even today, when I put bread in the toaster, when I fill the teapot, I am trying to make that same tea, that toast.

◆◆◆

Anyway, the sun shone brightly that day, from a wide, wide sky: the sea was liquid blue. A tractor moved slowly up and down a field on the far side of the loch, too far away to hear.

Once round the long bend of the beach, the shore became rocky and the cliffs began to encroach on the shore. At this point we usually turned up the hill, where the cliffs were easier to climb; smaller too, and there was thick heather at the base to break a fall.

◆◆◆

When I got a rod for my birthday, I spent hours getting the line tangled in the willows and the water-weeds.

Then you came along and caught six fish with my new rod. I went home empty-handed.

◆◆◆

But on this particular day, the tide was on the way out, so we carried on along the beach. Below the cliffs was a good place; here caves might hide Bonnie Prince Charlie's treasure, or human bones. We hunted for crabs, we fought battles. I tried to dislodge you from a fortress of rock. The day was endless. We went far beyond the furthest headland that we'd reached before. Our sandshoes got soaked dancing back from the waves, clothes and skin were rubbed thin on rock scrambles.

◆◆◆

We cycled all the way to Gruinard Bay once. My bike had a basket, so I collected the empty bottles the tourists had left behind. You lit a fire on the sand.

On the way home we ate the chocolate I bought with the bottles, and invented unlikely excuses for being late home.

It was the summer holidays. No-one had noticed we were gone.

◆◆◆

I found the pool and called you over. It was beautiful. Most rock pools are only a foot or two deep, but this was huge, five feet deep and ten feet across. Sandshoes came off, and we sat at the edge, splashing. It was a magical place. We both grew silent. I was fascinated by the water, so clear it was barely there except for the slight shimmer of sunlight and the giveaway waving of sea anemones and small water creatures.

◆◆◆

In the field behind your house, we began to dig a hole to Australia. The spade was too big for me, awkward to handle. We never finished it.

Years later, and I am a different person. I still dream sometimes that there is a secret cave behind the bush where we
dug.

◆◆◆

The rocks were warm, and the sun was hot. In the pool, the
shimmering of the water was hypnotic. We both wanted to go
in, but neither of us was sure how safe it was. As we talked
about it, the sun grew hotter. The water looked more and
more enticing, but the pool was deep and wide, and the sides
were steep.

'If you pushed off hard from this side you'd just sort of glide
across to the other side, where it's shallow.'

'Yeah, that would be great. I bet we could do that easy.'

'You wouldn't even have to be able to swim. You could
just float across.'

'Aye, people are lighter than water, aren't they?'

'Anyway, your toes would probably reach the bottom.'

Then I noticed something strange. I was talking about
whether *we* should do it. You were talking about whether *I*
should do it.

I fell quiet, and looked at the pool. It was deeper than my
height.

'Go on, you can do it.'

I looked up. Your eyes were eager.

'Go on.'

For no reason that I could think of, I remembered the look
on your face when you cut the tadpole's tail off.

That's when I said no.

# Plucking

The Landrover's light appeared, murky through the thickly falling snow. As it stopped, Dave shouldered his piece-bag and climbed in the back. There was no light in the back, and he fumbled for a seat.

'Here, Dave.' The voice was familiar. A soft hand took his and pulled him down onto the bench. To one side of him he could feel the rough cloth of an overcoat as one of the farm labourers moved up to make room for him. On the other side was a lighter, smoother cloth, and a half-familiar perfume.

As the details came together in his head, he suddenly felt almost paralysed by a mixture of self-consciousness and desire. It was Gina. Gina was a year older, and he saw her almost every day in school – but he'd never talked to her. She was always so easily casual, so sure of herself, so unattainable.

He managed to gulp out 'Thanks.' She squeezed his hand before releasing it. He thought he was going to melt.

'You leave that lad alone now, Gina. He's too young for the likes of you.' It was the rough voice of the farm manager, from the driver's seat.

There was a general chuckle from the figures in the darkness.

'We're going to be plucking turkeys, not...'

Another voice started singing, 'I'm not a pheasant plucker...'

Dave tried to pretend he was somewhere else, as the ribald laughter subsided and the Landrover began the long climb up the hill to the farm.

Dave stumbled into the brightly-lit shed. Most of the others worked during the week and knew the layout. They went to their stations, ready to start.

From a side room, one of the farm labourers emerged with a load of dead turkeys. He hung them up from hooks on a wire strung at about six feet high, and the men and women started plucking them.

Dave stood awkwardly by the main door, waiting to be told what to do.

'Hey, you there, what's-yer-name.' The farm manager beckoned him.

'Dave.'

'What's that?'

'My name. Dave'

The manager glared at him.

'All right, David. You go to the end here. You know the rates. 45p for each bird plucked. You get docked 10p if you tear the skin. Gina there will sew up any torn birds.'

Just beyond the door to the slaughtering room, Gina was standing, sharpening a small knife on a stone. Even as he looked, the first plucked turkey was hung before her, and she lifted her knife.

'Get to it.' The manager turned and left as the farm-hand hung up a turkey in front of Dave.

He began to pluck.

It was a slow business. The breast feathers were small, and came out easily, but there were so many of them. Soon the shed was filled with tiny swirling pieces of down. Dave's nose itched, but when he reached up to scratch it, more down stuck there.

The wing feathers were worst. At least with the breast it was possible to take it gently, and the back was easily stripped, but the main feathers were large and tough. They had to be pulled out by force. Dave's heart sank as the skin tore.

He got the bird as naked as he could, then glanced around helplessly to see what happened next. Gina came over with her needle and thread.

'You haven't done this before, have you?' She deftly began sewing up the tear.

'No.'

'Well, you're bound to tear a few. Just take it easy. If you twist these big feathers they come out more easily.'

'Thanks.'

Dave felt brainless and awkward. She was right there beside him, her thick black hair tied at the nape of her neck. He could see the rich red highlights in it as she bent over her work.

Why couldn't he think of anything to say?

'That's it.' She smiled, lifted the bird and took it to her station. Dave watched her as he waited for the next turkey. She took her small sharp knife and slit around the throat. Then she carefully cut around the bird's anus, underneath the parson's nose, and her small delicate hand reached up inside the bird. She gave one smooth pull, and all the innards came out and fell into a large stainless steel bucket.

Just then, the farm manager came up behind Gina and whispered something in her ear as he fondled her backside. Dave looked away.

In the side room, the farm hand was killing another turkey. Its feet had been tied together and it was passive as its head and neck were thrust into a bucket. The bucket had no bottom, but there was a lever there. The turkey's head stuck out, and its eyes blinked as Dave watched. Then the lever was pulled across, and the neck was broken.

'There you go, lad.' The man hung up the carcass on the hook, and Dave started pulling the feathers.

By the end of the day, Dave had plucked fifteen turkeys, and the last half-dozen had been done without a tear. He leaned against the shed in the twilight, feeling exhausted and depressed. The others were talking together in small groups as they waited for the Landrover, but Dave was silent and alone.

A band of light fell across the snow as the shed door opened again, and Gina came out. The manager was holding the door for her, and as she passed, he slapped her bottom and made a joke. Gina laughed. The door shut and the man went off to get the Landrover.

Dave stared morosely at his feet. He was thinking about whether to come back tomorrow. He needed the money, but not that much.

'You did all right today.' It was Gina.

'Just fifteen.' He didn't mention that half of them were torn.

'You're getting the hang of it. Another day or two and you'll start to pick up speed.'

Dave shrugged. Words had deserted him again. Her face was just visible in the growing dark, her perfume was fainter, and mixed with the smell of sweat. He was afraid to look at her. Every part of her seemed to be curved, each curve reaching towards him.

The headlights of the Landrover swept across them.

'Get in everyone. Hurry it up. Gina, you can get in the front seat with me. That'll keep you out of mischief.'

Gina's small hand pressed Dave's wrist once as she turned towards the vehicle.

Dave was waiting outside his home next morning. He disliked the work, but he did need the money. And there was Gina. Just the possibility of sitting next to her was enough to get him out of bed early on a Sunday morning and out into the snowy street.

This time though, he was less lucky. There was a seat just by the rear door, and he had to sit there beside the old woman who swept the shed. The vehicle lurched forward before he had a chance to sit down, and his head banged against the car body.

'Hey, steady on!' called one of the workers.

'You okay, son?' asked the old woman.

'I'm all right,' muttered Dave, holding the side of his head with his hand. He was sure the farm manager had done it deliberately.

The work went better. By lunchtime he had already plucked ten birds, only one of them torn. As he sat in the shed eating his sandwiches, Gina came over and sat by him.

'Can I sit here, Dave? Getting the hang of it now, aren't you?'

'Sure. Yes. I mean – yes, it's going all right.'

'What's up with your head?'

'What?' Dave had forgotten the knock.

She pointed.'There's a big bruise there.' Her small white hand rubbed his head gently. It was still painfully tender.

'Oh. I fell. In the Landrover.'

'Did you trip over something? I was in the front this morning.'

Dave felt awkward. He didn't want to sound like he was whingeing.

'It started too fast. He didn't give me a chance to sit down.'

'Oh.' She bit her lower lip, looked down. 'I'm sorry.'

'It's okay. Just an accident.' But he knew it wasn't, and so did she.

That afternoon, he watched her at her work. He was sure enough now of his job to pluck out the breast feathers in a snowstorm of down while he glanced up from time to time to see her, working away with her little knife. She smiled at him now and again, but he couldn't help turning away as her delicate white hand reached inside the turkey to empty it into the bucket.

The manager came past just once: he was busy elsewhere that day. When he tried to fondle Gina, she slapped his hand away. He laughed and passed by, checking the work.

Dave was back at school on Monday, but Gina had managed to get a sick note, and she would be working right up till Christmas Eve. Dave daydreamed about her in class, and in the bus on the way home; and at night too she came into his dreams.

Behind the town was a moorland, where Dave had used to play when he was younger. There were meandering streams and bogs up there, and he'd always been warned to stay away from these. So he was cautious. He would creep up to the mossy bog, and look at the way the sphagnum moss gradually dipped under the water away from the edges. In the centre it was deep and dark, and he could imagine that it just went on forever, so deep that you'd never reach the bottom if you fell in there.

In the centre, although it was dark, it was not completely black. The surface had a strong redness, a rust red, as if some strange essence of the peat, something like a vegetable blood, had stained it.

He dreamt about the bog one night, seeing its centre stained with red. He saw that the stain lay in threads and streams across the water, and then he saw that it was hair, dark hair, almost black, with rich red highlights in it. And there, in the centre of the hair, was Gina's face, smiling at him, welcoming him into the deepness, the darkness. As he woke from the dream, he could see her small white hand reaching out for him.

That weekend, there was another man driving the Landrover. There was no sign of the farm manager in the shed, either. The shed had been rearranged during the week to make room for more weekend workers, this close to Christmas. It was nearly lunchtime before he was absolutely sure that Gina was not there.

He didn't like to ask about Gina directly, but when the farm hand brought a fresh turkey he tried to strike up a conversation.

'Not seen the farm manager today.'

The man looked at him, grinned.

'Not likely to, neither. He's done a runner.'

'He's gone?'

'Yes, and all the loose cash on the farm too. We'll not see him again. Can't say I blame him – that wife of his is an old harridan.'

'He left his family behind?'

'Dead right. Ran off with that young lass – Gina. She used to gut the birds.'

'Oh.'

Dave turned to his turkey and began ripping the feathers out.

He quit at lunchtime, and walked home. There was a rain falling, melting the snow, leaving ragged patches of green in the white fields.

At the field gate he stopped, leaning against the cold metal. Raindrops cooled the back of his neck, where he had worked up a sweat. He gazed at the snow on the ground. It was melting fast now. By his sodden boot a lump of slush dissolved into the stream of water flowing out into the road.

He sighed and relaxed, enjoying the quiet patter of the rain, the gurgle of the stream. Enjoying the unexpected feeling of relief.

# Stubble

When I first met Derek, I was instantly on my guard. He looked tough – he had a strut and he had a curl to his lip. He also had painfully short hair. The skinned-animal look of his skull frightened and repelled me. Then he spoke. A long deep drawl elongated itself from his mouth: an exaggerated pansy's voice. Plainly, he was just a hollow man, and given a choice I would never even have talked to him.

Unfortunately, we were forced together. We were both employed digging drainage ditches for forestry planting. There was only one place to drink in that corner of Mull: the Kinloch Hotel. The pub was so small that five people made an instant party. You couldn't ignore anyone. Sometimes it was great. Sometimes it wasn't. One night, in a room no bigger than a scullery, we had sixteen people, and one of them was playing the bagpipes.

Derek was at the back, on the raised bench, against the wall. When it was his turn to buy a round, he stood up and flapped a hand at the barman.

'Donnie, dee-a-r. Donnie!' His fluting bass voice cut right through the bar-room noise, including the pipes, and Donnie turned. 'Three pints of heavy, Donnie dear, and two Old Tobermories. Thanks, pet.'

He passed a ten-pound note forwards, hand to hand until it reached the bar. His change, and then the drinks, came back by the same route.

The hillside was that endless dreary dun brown of fuck-all-but-heather, with occasional patches of greeny brown that meant there was bog there. We had rutters and heughs to work with. The heugh was like a garden fork with the prongs turned forwards. The rutter was a huge unwieldy spade. We had to carry a file to keep it sharp. The file was called a half-round bastard, a name which lost its humorous quality by the end of the first week. We had waterproofs, welly boots, flasks and food for the day. There were no nearby roads, so before we started work we had a three-mile walk-in with our half-hundredweight of equipment.

'Jottered before you even start,' was Graham's comment, the first day. I tried leaving my tools on the hillside, to save carrying them in, but then we got moved to another hill mid-week, so I had to spend a couple of hours retrieving my kit. After that, I carried my tools in and out each day.

Derek was sympathetic. 'I did the same thing, dear. My little legs were so tired that first week!'

There was something arresting about his voice, rumbling and feminine at the same time. It was horrifying and fascinating: I couldn't turn away; I couldn't ignore him.

How do you end up in a job like that? Some of the workers were forestry students, there for the summer. They had college to go back to, with a job in forest management at the end of the course. Most of the rest of us were in need of money, cash in hand, no questions asked. This was paid at the end of the week, after the boss had paced out the length of the ditches we'd cut. It was piece-work: no ditches, no money.

We lived in a collection of old caravans that smelled of damp and tobacco and unwashed socks. There was no promotion ladder out of here. You just got good at digging ditches or you quit and slipped down another snake on the playing board.

Derek was different, of course. He had a wee house on the peninsula of Ardnamurchan and he worked on the forestry for cash to keep his croft running. How he managed, with his unmistakeably homosexual voice, among the good Christian folk of Ardnamurchan, I don't know. The Kirk are not noted for their tolerance of deviants.

One night of storms and heavy rain, we had a flood in the Kinloch bar. Coming down from my caravan at about eight in the evening, I noticed that the water was high under the bridge. The sun was down, but there was enough light to show an extraordinary sight along the hillsides. The wind, in from the west, was blowing with such force that some of the burns were being driven back uphill. Along the far side of the glen, the water could not even fall down the cliffs – when the streams reached the edge, they were blown straight up into the sky.

It was hard work, struggling down the road against the wind and driving rain, but the warmth of the bar called to me. Behind me was the boom and rattle of the caravan, shaken by the wind. Its gas heater gave out a damp heat: warmth without comfort. I wanted people and noise and drink. The light was going fast, and I fell through the doorway of the bar with a feeling of relief.

'Oh, Colin, you're looking wet, dear. Come on over here.'

Derek moved over, to give me his seat by the fire. There was no-one else in the bar and I could hardly refuse.

'Did you see the fountains?' he asked.

'Fountains?'

'Yes, dear. Fountains. Where the wind is blowing the streams into the air.'

'Oh aye. I saw that,' I snorted. 'So the rain's falling twice.'

'That's very good, dear,' he said in an appreciative voice. 'Worth a drink, in my humble opinion. Barman! An Old Tobermory and a pint of heavy for this perceptive and witty young man.'

Donnie raised his eyebrows at this, but poured the drinks. I blushed. The door opened and Graham came in.

'By god, did you see the hillsides? The streams are going right up in the bloody air!'

'Yes,' said Derek. 'So the rain's falling twice!'

Graham looked baffled for a second, then he barked out a laugh. 'Aye! That's just what it feels like too!'

Derek simpered at me and winked. 'You see,' he said. 'I told you. Now drink up that whisky before you catch a chill.'

He stroked his close-cropped head in an uncomfortably sensual way, his eyes on mine, then turned away to talk with Graham.

Eventually there were six of us in there, a fair complement for such a night, and every one of us part of the captive clientèle from the caravan emplacement on the hillside two hundred yards up the road. We were all aware that we were here for solace, for company. For refuge from the flimsy temporary shelters where we'd have to sleep.

The owner of the Kinloch knew our circumstances and was happy to let Donnie serve us for as long as we had the inclination and the money to remain. That night, it looked set fair for a two a.m. closing time. I knew I could last two more rounds before my cash ran out – and I had no intention of leaving before that point.

But that amount of beer has to go somewhere, and we all had to visit the toilet regularly. One oddity of the Kinloch was that the bar had no indoor toilet. There was a urinal in a shed at the back of the hotel: basically a tiled wall with a gutter along the floor at the bottom of it. Crude but perfectly adequate, for men at least. Ladies had other arrangements.

Graham was telling a story about catching a chicken with the side-door of his camper van. When he'd finished and we'd all appreciated it, he rose and announced that he was going out back. 'Jesus Christ!' he said as he opened the door. Then gingerly he stepped out and pulled the door shut.

He was laughing when he returned.

'I went for a pee,' he said, 'but the path was underwater. I've got my wellies on, so I just waded round the back. Would you believe it, the toilet's got six inches of water in it too! But I didn't care. Not me, with my wellies on. I just waded on through to the urinal. So there I was, standing in front of the tiled wall, John Thomas hanging out, and I realise that I'm standing in a bloody pond, carefully pissing into the bit of water that's covering the urinal!'

The owner came through from the hotel to see what the laughter was all about.

'Och, it's just Graham,' said the barman. 'He was telling us there's water in the toilet.'

'Of course there is.' The manager frowned and looked around, waiting to be told what was so funny about that. 'It wouldn't be much of a toilet if there was no water.'

'Nah, nah,' said Graham. 'Lots of water.' Seeing that the

manager still didn't understand, he stood up and turned the door handle. 'Like this.'

The wind caught the door and flung it back. Water gushed in. In a moment, the bar was half-flooded and the manager was shouting and swearing.

'Shut the bloody door! Donnie, get a mop and a bucket. A bucket, you eejit, quick!'

Graham, crippled with laughter, tried to force the door shut, but needed help against the wind and the water. Even then, water still purled in at the edges. Donnie was swearing back at the manager now. 'A bucket's no fucking good! It's a flood, for Christ's sake!'

The owner was still trying to make the water go away by shouting. He turned on us. 'And what the fuck are you lot doing here anyway? It's after bloody midnight!'

'We're drinking, darling,' said Derek. 'Could I have another pint of eighty shilling, please?'

The lights went out. The water had not yet reached the log fire in the grate, so we all sat in an orange glow, the firelight reflecting off the rippling water.

'Oh shit, that's the fuses blown now!'

'So there's no chance of another pint then?'

'Of course there's not, you stupid great poofter! The pumps won't work!'

'Oh dear,' sighed Derek. 'It'll have to be a nip of Old Tobermory, then.'

The storm was audible, even from inside the bar, but it had been largely muffled by the walls – and by the heavy drinking. Outside, it was a maelstrom. We huddled together for safety as we went along the road in the pitch dark and past the bridge. That was where all the water was coming from, the burn. Our ditches were draining the hillsides so fast that the river bed couldn't hold it. The bridge itself was gushing with water, tumbling over the parapet – we had to link arms to get across it, mostly by feel, banging and crashing against the low stone walls, only that way knowing which direction to go.

After that, we turned up the hillside, skidding on the mud

and sodden grass. Up ahead, a dim light gleamed.

'That's my caravan!' Derek yelled. 'Head that way!'

We couldn't go straight up the hill. The wind caught us and blew us sideways until we came up against the fence. Then we pulled ourselves along it. First Graham, then each of the others headed off to their bunks, until there was only Derek and I, crawling our way along the edge of the field.

We reached Derek's caravan and he shouted, 'Can you find yours?'

'I'll be fine,' I shouted back.

'Without lights?'

'I think so!'

'I'll come with you!'

'No, it's okay!'

He didn't argue. He grabbed my arm and pulled. We scrambled farther along the fence.

'Are we there yet?'

His hand was still on my arm. I nodded, then shouted, 'Yes!'

'Let's go, then!'

We let go of the fence and headed out into the field. I had my arms outstretched, so I didn't crash into the caravan, but it was so dark that neither of us could find it. We went back to the fence, then tried again. No caravan, but I cracked my shin on something and fell over onto the saturated hillside. I clutched at my leg. 'Bastard! Bastard!'

I could hear Derek shouting, but couldn't make out the words. I shouted back and his voice came closer.

'You okay?'

'I fell over something!'

'A stone?'

'No!' I fumbled around. 'Something metal! Here it is!'

'What is it?'

'I don't know! Wait a minute, it's … it's my gas cylinder!'

'By itself?'

'Yes! It must have blown away!'

There was a long silence from Derek and me, though the gale howled around us and wet clothing rippled and snapped in the wind.

'I don't think so,' said Derek. He was right beside me now. 'Your caravan's gone.'

I sat, huddled by the gas heater, absorbing warmth and light, while Derek's caravan shook and trembled. The gale moaned as it tried to grip the wheels, the windows, the door. Derek was working over his tiny stove trying to get hot coffee together.

I was in shock. I had stopped completely, as if my spring had run down. My mind was empty except for what fell into it: warm light and Derek's face, gaunt and soaked, glowing in the light from the gas mantles on the wall. He turned to look at me now and then, and grinned. My face was so cold I couldn't even smile back at him. He gave me coffee and I spilled it down my front. My hands were shaking.

'What, what, what,' I said.

'What?'

'The caravan.'

'This caravan?'

I nodded.

'It's tied down. I did it myself. Wired to stakes in the ground. Boulders on the stakes. We'll be fine.'

I finally managed to smile. 'Thanks, Derek,' I said. 'Thank you.'

'Oh, it's nothing, dear,' he said, fussily, and I realized that his camp voice was back, and I'd never even noticed that it was gone. 'You'll have to sleep on the floor, sweetie, unless,' and one of his eyebrows raised, 'Unless you'd like to share...?' He glanced at his own bed, then back at me.

I managed half a smile. 'Thanks, Derek, but no thanks.'

His lower lip pouted. 'It's just for the sake of warmth. But please yourself. Here's your bedding. I'm off to bed. Alone.'

He threw a couple of blankets on the floor, stripped off his wet clothing and climbed into bed.

I laid out the blankets, undressed, then dimmed the gas light.

'Hey, Derek,' I said.

'Yes.' He gave the word three syllables and managed to

23

make it sound sulky. His head was turned to the wall and the light gleamed dimly on the short fuzz on his skull.

'Sorry, but I have to do this.' I reached out and brushed my hand over his head, as if I was stroking an animal. It felt soft and bristly, both at the same time. 'I didn't mean anything by that,' I said.

'I know,' he replied, and the sulkiness was gone from his voice.

I rolled myself into my blankets.

'Good night,' he said.

'Good night,' I said.

## Under the Hawthorn

Down the path straggled the line of children, with Andrew near the end. They were playing at gangs. Some of them carried wooden swords, some had dustbin lids that they used for shields. The youngest ones just had sticks, while the oldest of them all had both a sword and a shield. He was the leader.

He was nearly five.

On the left of the path was a high wall with the roofs of tenement blocks just visible over the top. There were doors in the wall every few yards, red or blue, with flaking paint.

To the right was a line of trees along a bank at the back of a row of gardens. As he marched along, Andrew whacked the trees with his stick. Like most of the younger children, he didn't know what was going on, but he was happy to join in.

As they marched along, Andrew began to fall behind, his attention taken by small plants, interesting stones, movements in the grass. At the top of the bank was a hawthorn bush. There was a path up to it and there was a clear area under the branches, worn by many children using it as a den. The gnarled trunk was polished by the touch of their hands.

Andrew thought he saw movement under the bush. He stopped. Even here in the town, rabbits were sometimes found. He glanced along the path to see where the other children were. They were quite distant now, and he would have to run if he wanted to catch them up. He turned and climbed up the bank. He was sure now that it had been a rabbit that he'd seen. He crawled around under the bush, looking.

He found no trace of the rabbit, but this sheltered place was thick with the smell of hawthorn blossom, and by now the sound of the other children was faint. He lay back against the trunk, gouging the dry earth with his stick and shaping the soil into little heaps and lines.

There was a far-off hum of traffic and now and then a snatch of birdsong. He sang small nonsense to himself, rocking to and fro. He felt warm and safe.

The sound of a man's heavy footsteps came along the path, stumbling from time to time. He was hidden by the trees. Andrew leaned forward to see who was coming. The footsteps became louder and the man could be heard muttering to himself.

As the man appeared round the trunk of a tree, he and Andrew saw one another simultaneously. The man stopped, startled, then recognised the boy.

'Andrew!'

'Hello, Mr. Maplin.'

It was the man who lived up the stair. His face was red and his eyes were bright.

Whenever she saw him like that, Andrew's mum would sniff and say, 'Drinking again. Fine way for a teacher to behave!' But only after Mr. Maplin had passed by.

'That's a grand wee den you've got there.'

Andrew said nothing. Mr. Maplin was looking at him closely. He licked his moist red lips and glanced up and down the path.

'Well-hidden, too, eh? A fine den.' He moved closer and took a couple of steps up the bank. Andrew could smell the drink on his breath now, hear his ragged breathing.

'Now, lad, there's something I want to show you. It's a secret, mind, and you've not to tell.' He was fumbling with the zipper on his trousers. Andrew was transfixed as the man drew closer, pulling his trousers open, pulling his swollen penis out, stroking it as he moved toward the boy.

'Look at that, now. Have you ever seen the like?'

Andrew was unable to move his eyes from the man's penis, waving to and fro as he came closer and closer.

'Now, wouldn't you like to touch that now, wouldn't you like to give that... Aargh! Oh shit!'

Advancing almost blindly towards the boy, the sharp spines of the hawthorn had taken him full in the face. He staggered back, hands to his face.

'Holy shit! It's taken the eye out of me!'

A door opened in the wall across the road. A woman's voice spoke. 'Is that you, Mr. Maplin? Are you all right?'

The man had the presence of mind not to turn round. He backed his way down the bank, doubled over to hide the front of his trousers. 'Just fine, just fine. Caught myself on the bush there.'

While talking, he was edging his way on to the path, keeping his back to the woman, holding one hand to his face, trying to fumble himself back into his trousers with the other hand.

'Are you sure you're all right? Is there anything I can...'

'No, no. Thank you, I'm perfectly fine...' He stumbled off, still bent over, trying to keep up his end of the conversation, 'Very kind of you ... but no, I'm all right now...' unaware that the woman had fallen silent and was standing still, staring after him.

As Mr. Maplin reached the corner and was lost to sight, she turned to the hawthorn bush and saw Andrew for the first time. He had withdrawn into himself and was sitting there with his thumb in his mouth.

'What are you doing there?' she asked sharply. 'Up to no good, I'll be bound. Get along home now!" Andrew sat there unmoving. 'Come on!' She moved up the bank towards him, holding out her hand. Andrew took hold of it, stood up.

'He didn't do anything, did he?' Andrew looked at her silently. 'Nothing bad?' He didn't reply. She sighed, and led him down the road.

She took Andrew home, and handed him to his mother at the door. 'Found this one under a bush.' She considered whether to say any more. 'Better keep an eye on him.'

'And what do you mean by that?'

'There's folk around here that shouldn't be left alone with children.' She nodded towards the upper storey where Mr. Maplin lived.

Andrew's mother refused to acknowledge the warning.

'Thank you very much. I think I know how to take care of my own child.'

The other woman left in a huff.

Andrew spent the rest of the day indoors, curled in a chair. His mother was afraid he was ill. She brought him a blanket, and food, which he hardly touched.

He lay there thinking.

There was a walk that he went often with his mum. They took his baby sister in the pram, to the medical centre. It was a long walk, and he'd always liked it. It had a pleasant pattern to it and different places to see on the route.

First they walked down the street, slowly, stopping to speak to folk and to pat the dog that always lay by the gate. Then they turned the corner, and the road dipped to go under the railway bridge. It was always cold and damp: the sunlight never reached here, and there were strange smells. They walked through quickly, then out into the open air.

Next, there was the field, a small one with a donkey in it. They walked slowly here, talking about the donkey. It was just like the little plastic one he had in his farm set. After the field they came to the waste land, where a bomb had landed in the war, long ago. It had never been cleared, and it was a jumble of broken masonry and concrete. There was nothing interesting to talk about, and they went fast here, until they reached the street where the Centre was.

One day, walking past the field, he'd noticed something different. The donkey didn't look just like the toy one at home. There was something underneath it.

'Mum, what's that on the donkey?'

She glanced over. 'There's nothing on the donkey, dear.'

'Not on its back, Mum. Under its back, there.' He pointed. The donkey's penis hung, swollen and nearly as long as its tail, swaying from side to side as the donkey rubbed itself against the corner post.

She looked straight ahead and started walking faster.

'Come along now, we're late. We haven't all day, you know.'

'But, Mum...'

'Come on!'

On the way home, he waited eagerly for the field. The donkey's erection had not subsided.

'There, Mum! That's it. What is it?'

She didn't look. 'Probably its tail. Hurry up.'

From that day, the walk lost its pleasure. The patterns changed. His mum grew apprehensive as they reached the end of the street. They went under the bridge quite slowly now, then rushed past the donkey field, with no time to ask questions. They only slowed again when they reached the waste land.

Lying there on the chair, Andrew began to put things together. His mum got upset when he didn't do up the buttons on the front of his trousers. And she told him not to play with his thing. And he had to shut the door when he was using the toilet: though his father didn't always, and she would tell him off, too.

And why didn't he have any names for that part of his body? The other boys had names for that part, but he wasn't allowed to use the words at home or his mum would get angry.

He began to realize that there was something wrong, something bad about that bit. The donkey that had changed their walk had a big bit there. So did Mr. Maplin.

He felt worse and worse, afraid of some badness that he hadn't caused and could do nothing about. And he couldn't ask, because it was so bad that he wasn't even allowed to talk about it.

In a panic, he struggled up and ran out of the room, down the corridor to the bathroom. He closed the door and managed to push the bolt shut. He pushed down his trousers and bent over to look. It didn't look like anything dreadful. As he looked, he began to relax.

He thought about Mr. Maplin, and looked at his own thing. It was very small.

He thought about the donkey, and looked at himself again. It was tiny.

He didn't feel so bad any more. It was so small that it probably wouldn't matter.

Still, before he left the bathroom, he carefully buttoned up his flies.

# Bardo Thodol

The kitchen door opens and Dad sticks his head in.
'It's time.'

I put my cards down, reluctantly. Dad beckons. I stand up.
Govinda reaches across the table and sorts through my cards
to see what I'd been holding. He picks up Mrs Bun and looks
disgusted.

'You had it!'

The other children are not sorry to see me go. I won the last
five games and I'm fed up with Happy Families. Trouble is, little
Mary's too young for anything else. Hamily was ready to quit
too. She doesn't like losing, and she'd been getting spiteful.

I can hear Dad's footsteps on the stairs.

'Don't dawdle,' says Mum. I sigh and follow Dad.

Upstairs, the door is open and the room looks dim after
the bright light in the kitchen. I step into the warmth and the
disturbing bedroom smells. Disturbing because it's female, but
not my mother or sister. Disturbing because it is the smell of
a sick-bed.

Once inside, the candles are dazzling. Dad gestures to the
shadows, where there is a wooden chair. I sit as comfortably
as I can, looking curiously around at the statuette on the
mantelpiece, the pictures on the wall, the curtain. Aunt Padma
standing by the head of the bed.

Dad settles on his stool and opens the book he has been
carrying. He lays it in his lap. He waits. Padma dampens a cloth
in a bowl of water and leans over the bed. One candle near the
window is flickering. I can see a dribble of wax running down
its side. There is silence.

I have nothing left to look at and the silence continues. My
gaze keeps slipping away from things, drifting round towards
the bed. I give in and look.

I'd expected her face to have changed, to be older, wrinkled,
thinner. I'd been imagining it in the kitchen, so that now it
would have been a shock to see her healthy.

But the shock now is to see how little of her still remains in the face. It is shrunken and fallen-in – and empty.

Her eyes roll sideways to look at me. I freeze, don't know what to do.

Then Dad speaks and I jump in my seat. 'Didi, he is here. As witness to your going, if this is acceptable.'

Her lips part. 'Yes,' she says, clearly. 'I am pleased.' Her head moves slightly, an attempt at a nod.

'Now it is the hour of your death. It is time for you to pass from this world. Do you understand?'

'I understand.'

'Then it is time for you to find the Path.'

I hate it when he sounds so solemn. I wriggle in my seat. His eyes turn to me briefly. I sit still. He begins an invocation, calling on gods and spirits to circle us round, to keep the place safe. I have heard them before, so I listen to Didi's breath, listen to what is left of her life.

◆◆◆

The candles have burned low and are beginning to flicker. At the end of an incantation, Dad asks me quietly to change them. I go round, lighting a new candle from each old one and replacing it in the candlestick.

I am glad to be moving. When I stood up, my back ached and my legs had pins and needles.

Dad has been reciting for hours, not looking at the book, but keeping it in his lap. I'm sorry that Didi is dying, terribly sorry, but I wish I was somewhere else. Even in the kitchen with the stupid card game and Hamily's bad temper.

The thing with Hamily is, she particularly dislikes losing at cards to me, since she is only a year younger. I wish I was a year younger too. Then I wouldn't be up here with Padma and Dad and Didi. I can't see why I have to be here.

Then Didi's breathing changes, just a tiny change, and suddenly I am paying attention. Didi's life is ending. That's why I am here.

Dad's voice has changed too. He has been waiting for this moment and now he is poised and alert.

31

'Just let go, Didi, let go. Let it happen.'

Didi's pale face glows in the candlelight. 'I feel so heavy,' she whispers. 'Like a great clod of earth.' Her eyes open, then close again. 'Sinking…'

'Earth sinking into water. The first stage of death.' Dad is so sure, as if he's right there with her. In her mind.

Padma has her eyes closed, but her body is poised, paying attention.

Dad continues to recite.

'Let go now, and go to that place between this life and the next. Do not tarry, look for the great light of that in-between place.'

The in-between place. There must be a better word. Death, of course, is the obvious one but that isn't really what he means – it is too final.

Of course, for us, her death is final. Probably. Didi would die and not be seen again.

But something of Didi would be reborn… Or perhaps not. I really don't know. She is speaking again, her voice very low.

'Cold now. Cold.'

'Didi, the time is coming for you to find the Path into Reality.'

You can hear the Capital Letters. Sometimes it seems so contrived, when he speaks like that. Does he know he's doing it? Maybe one day I'll say the words the same. With a shock, I realize that this is the first time I've ever thought that I might do this, do the job that Dad does.

'Soon you will see the Great Light; you must experience it in Reality where all things are void and empty.'

'I'm all hot. Burning up.'

'Good. Water sinking into fire. Now you have passed through the second stage of death. All is as it should be.'

He sounds so confident, so sure. Not just about the stages of death – of course he knows them. He's seen that in other people. But he's sure also about what she's going to encounter beyond this life. They say some people can remember what it's like, from a previous life. Perhaps he does – or is it just what he's read?

It would feel good to be sure of things. To know that they're there, the Gods that protect the Dharma. Even the Demons that are their dark side. Thing is, it's a recorded doctrine that Gods and Demons are constructs of the mind. Buddha said so.

Dad says so too. He also says they're real, as well, and I can't quite grasp that. He can't have it both ways. It would be nice though, if they were real. Not for the comfort, though it would be good to know that there were other conscious beings around. No, not for the companionship. Just because then I'd know where I was. What the world was really like.

He's reading again. 'And at this point, know yourself as boundless and empty, and abide in that state.'

Now he starts at the beginning again, repeating it over and over until the right moment arrives. I have to wait and watch. He wants me to know all about it. I suppose I do too, but it's not easy. It would be a lot easier to be downstairs playing cards, but Dad says I'm old enough.

So I'm sitting here, trying to keep my attention on the moment in case it happens just now, while my bottom grows sweaty and sticks to the wooden chair. When it's time to move I'll have to peel myself off slowly, getting up like an old man.

I move slightly to ease myself, but of course Dad's eyes flicker to me and back again. He's got this whole room in his attention, keeping us all focused on Didi as she goes.

Didi's face is blank now. Her eyes are open but not looking at anything. Nothing in the room anyway. Her breath comes in small gasps. She speaks, very quietly.

'Falling…' she says. 'Falling apart…'

Dad nods.

'Into … into … atoms.'

'Fire sinking into air,' says Dad. A hint of a smile on his face now, gentle.

'Atoms of light…'

Her breath is so faint now, I can hardly see the sheet moving over her breast.

'Noble one,' Dad says, 'don't let your mind be distracted. Didi, death having arrived, think to yourself: by using this death to advantage I will help all beings. Directing myself to

33

the Perfect Light, I will attain that perfection.

'You are about to cease breathing. With your breath, let all attachments fall from your mind. Let your mind be transparent, without a centre, without an edge.'

He is silent, while Didi's breath fades away. One of the candles is letting a thread of smoke into the air. Nothing else is moving in the room.

'Know now that the naked consciousness which you have become is the Clear Light.'

The candlelight gleams on Didi's face, lying there on the white pillow, empty. Padma is poised by the bedside, watching her. I am leaning forward, watching Didi's eyes. The candlelight is a small gleam in the darkness of her eyes. A tiny flame in a well, dropping towards the black water, fading as it falls, so that it is not possible to tell when it finally goes out.

When Padma moves I sit up and snort. Thick candle smoke is drifting across my face. Dad doesn't rebuke me. He is turning to another section of the book. Padma is turning from the bed. Folding the damp cloth, picking up the bowl of water from the bedside table.

Didi's body on the bed is empty now. I ease myself from the chair. Dad looks at me and nods. I pinch off the drooping candle wick before I cross to the door and leave. Behind me, I can hear Dad beginning the next set, reciting the words over Didi's dead body.

'O Didi, now fasten before you the image of the perfected Being. Let this Being stand before you as it were the moon on water, apparent but not existing...'

In the kitchen, the children turn to me, not asking the question they want to ask. They have been drawing at the table, to keep them quiet. Mother is chopping vegetables. She turns to me, nodding her head, not asking that question, because she knows. But still looking at me. Wanting the answer to another question.

'She's gone.' I say.

The children look upset, shocked or curious, depending on their ages.

Hamily puts her head down. Her long dark hair covers her face. Her body begins to shake. I wonder for a moment if she is cold, before I realise that she is crying.

I turn to mother. She is watching me, can see the puzzlement in my face. She nods again, satisfied. She glances towards Hamily.

I go over to Hamily, lean down and put an arm around her. She turns and puts her face against my chest. I can feel her sobs going into me, falling into a deep pool, where the ripples fade away.

# Looking for the Spark

# Looking For The Spark

Where the road is straight, he lifts his tin from the dash-board. He is steering with his forearms resting on the wheel, his face not far from the windscreen. Gusts of wind batter at the van, but we barely drift from a straight line. Below his chin, his fingers pry open the tin, select a cigarette paper and a pinch of tobacco.

From my seat I can see his eyes concentrating solely on the road ahead, while his fingers carefully hold the makings so that any excess tobacco falls into the tin held between his palms. The skin of his palms is smooth, slightly glossy from the constant friction of the safety gloves. When I check my own hands, they are rough, prickled with a thousand tiny abrasions from the spruce needles and bark. I rub my cheek with one hand. The hand feels bristly, as if it needs a shave.

He was in no way different from other men. When he drove a fence-post, he lifted the mell as other men do, pausing at the top of the swing and letting it drop. He did it well, raising himself on his toes at the last moment so that the face of the mell landed flat on the top of the post. The fence-post rang as he struck and the earth swallowed another few inches of wood.

When you're fencing, you never go anywhere with empty hands. There's always something to carry up or down the line of the fence. After the first few days you learn. Sometimes you see someone start off, then remember and pick up a roll of wire or a mell. With the more experienced men it shows as just a moment's hesitation.

The squad worked better when he was there, even though he wasn't the foreman. When he had set a post, he never paused: just shouldered the mell, picked up a couple of posts, or what-ever was needed, and was off to the next post-hole. The rest of us automatically worked around him, letting him set the pace.

By the time we reach the corner, he has placed the tobacco in the paper and closed the tin. He drops it back on the dash-board and sits up, both hands on the wheel, the paper pinched closed on the tobacco between his index and middle fingers. A shred of tobacco hangs out at one end, rocks to and fro in the draught from the air vent. After the corner, there is a short straight stretch. His wrists rest on the steering wheel, he rolls the cigarette, lifts and licks it, rolls it closed and puts it between his lips, presses in the cigarette lighter. Turns into the bend.

Nor is he unusual in any other way. He shops for himself, buys clothes and food. Perhaps he watches television in the evening. I have seen him in the crowded streets on Saturday afternoon, completely unremarkable among the other shoppers. I barely notice that I've noticed him, until afterwards. Other people too move through crowds without being jostled or impeded. It is a skill most people learn, after a while.

Now and then I have seen him in the bar, drinking lager, speaking with the barman, playing pool with his friends, whom I know only by sight. He inhabits a world that is not the same as mine, though they overlap. It's not a large community: I've heard his friends talking, seen them now and then at work. They're a mixed bunch, but none of them are remarkable. None of them is interesting in the way that he is, for all his ordinariness.

The lighter clicks and he lifts it to the cigarette, inhales, blows out blue mist. Though I do not smoke, I enjoy the smell of the tobacco smoke mingling with the petrol and oil and the scent of spruce resin and pine sap.

My eyes flicker open and closed. I lapse into a warm doze, unexpectedly satisfied with getting the day's work done, getting the contract finished. Somehow it's more than just labouring when you can see the size of the job, when you can aim your-self at the end of it. I know he's got nothing lined up for next week. My eyes are half-closed, but I can see his face. He's not worried. I don't know if I'll find work anywhere else, but I'm not worried either. It must be contagious.

He was cutting a ride through a plantation. I was working to him with the hook, stacking the pulp and the saw logs. The work was hard, the day was hot.

The tree shivered, he pulled the saw out, stepped to one side and it fell. Before the branches had stilled, he was trimming the trunk: brown dead twigs near the base, then thicker green branches towards the top. He sliced the top off and I stepped in with the hook, stumbling on the hag, and turned the tree. He worked down again, trimming the branches which had been underneath. Then he hooked his tape-measure on the end, walked along, marking the tree in three-metre sections, then turned and walked back, cutting the tree into pulp logs, while his tape rewound itself. He bent down and unhooked the tape and moved onto the next tree. I dashed in and hauled the logs into a more-or-less neat pile at the side of the ride.

I was doing the unskilled job. Hauling logs across a horrible bouncing mattress of branches lying on rough ground riddled with dead stumps and drainage ditches. And every log was different. The lie of the hag changed with every tree that came down. Logs snagged on a stump or rolled the wrong way. If the stack wasn't right, it could collapse when the new log went on it.

But he had an easy rhythm to his work, going through the same motions again and again, every tree the same. Cut it down, walk once up and down the fallen tree to sned the branches, once up and down to cut it into lengths, then on to the next tree.

Of course, when I tried it myself, I found it took some skill to make the job so dull and predictable. A breeze was enough to send a tree sideways. A first cut that was a centimetre too deep would jam the sawblade. And if it fell backwards into the other trees, it had to be cut down into useless logs, a few feet at a time.

There was nothing remarkable in the way he felled trees. That was a difficult skill to master.

By the time he finishes his cigarette, we are coming down the hill, and I am busy planning what will happen when I get home. It's Friday night and I'm feeling good that we finished the job just at the week's end. There should be good crack at the National tonight, they've got a band on. And Martin's back from the West. There will be a party at his place.

'There's a party up the Heights tonight.'

'Aye?' He acknowledges the statement.

We're coming up to the main road now. He watches the road as he stubs his cigarette out. His face is attentive, he checks both ways. There's nothing to say. He does not speak.

One morning, he didn't arrive to pick me up. I had no phone, so I walked out to his house. He had the engine out of his van and was taking it to pieces.

'Wasn't sounding right,' he said. 'Be a couple of hours.'

I stayed to help, but there wasn't much for me to do. He didn't work fast: he took time to select the right tool for each job, laying the engine parts in a semi-circle around him.

I remember when we dismantled an engine at school, I had an uneasy feeling that something was missing. All the parts were there, shiny metal bits that slid against each other or spun round each other, but there didn't seem to be anything to make it go. I tried asking the teacher, but he didn't understand that I was looking for some sort of final cause: he lectured me on the expansion of gases. Then I noticed the spark plugs, lying on a bench, and the pieces came together. That was the important bit, the spark that made it go.

As he delved deeper into the van engine, something of the same feeling came back to me. This was a diesel engine. It didn't have a spark plug. I understood well enough that the explosion of fuel and air was caused by sudden compression, but that wasn't a final cause.

When all the bits were spread out, naked and shining, I asked him.

'Where's the bit that makes it go?'

He looked surprised for a moment and I thought he was going to tell me about explosive compression. But he didn't.

'You start it moving and it keeps going,' he said. That didn't help. He must have seen it in my face. He shrugged. 'It goes

42

because it goes.'

That was it. I could grasp that. The core secret of the diesel engine.

'Right.'

He gathered some pieces of engine and began to put them together again, without hurry, but wasting no time.

I wonder what he does at home. Whether it is different from other people that I know. Whether it is unusual, or even interesting.

I imagine it is quite ordinary. There is no local gossip about him and I don't think his relatives live here. Though they might do. If they were as unremarkable as he is, perhaps no-one would know.

I watch him, try to imagine him with a brother or a sister. He concentrates on the road, anticipating the traffic well to keep the old van moving smoothly.

We worked for an hour at a time, until his petrol ran out and we stopped to refill. I needed the five minutes rest. He cleaned his saw and sharpened the chain.

It was late in the day and I was tired. I couldn't walk on the hag without stumbling, jamming one leg and then the other amongst the layers of branches. After a short break, he started back along the ride, studying the next tree, while his feet stepped over the snarly branches, avoided the hidden gaps. Landing always on a solid place.

I knew I should move. If he started on a second tree before I cleared the first, I'd have to hook the logs out from under. But I couldn't do it. We'd been working since 5 a.m. to get the cool of the day. I'd stripped down to T-shirt and shorts and my fore-arms and legs were scraped and bleeding and needle-pricked. My face was burning hot and stinging with perspiration.

He stopped at the tree and started up the chain-saw. He leant over to cut, but before he began, he looked to see where I was. He stood up again, his head shaking. It was too far away to be sure, but I think he was grinning. He beckoned me to come on and I stood up. He bent and started the cut.

Before I began moving down the ride I stood for a moment and looked. The spruce needles in the canopy were a dark blue-green from underneath, but where the cut branches lay on the ground, the upper part of the needles was visible, a brighter emerald green. There was a blue stripe of sky above the ride, bordered with dark blue-green. Below, there was a brown-walled corridor of tree trunks and a broad bright carpet of emerald green leading to the next tree, where he was a small figure intent on his work.

I stumbled forward on the hag and my mind swallowed the image whole.

We're stopping now. He opens the glove compartment, gets out his wallet, counts money onto his knee then hands it to me.

I take the money and check it, because I should, but not really counting. He's reliable.

I stow the money away. The engine is running. I climb out and wave.

He waves back and drives off. There is nothing remarkable about his going.

# On The Dragon

It was a stone ridge pushing through the soil. There was thin turf on top of it, but the sides were bare rock. The dragon's bones, we called it, from its shape. On sunny days it seemed about ready to awake – but it never did.

Mairi and I lay together on top of it and looked at the cars coming along Shore Road. Usually, one or two cars would pass in an hour, but when there was something special on, like a funeral, there was a constant stream. People came from far-off for a funeral or a wedding. Or communion. That only happened once or twice a year, so everyone came to the church for that.

Today it was a funeral and there was a particular pleasure on a day like today in lying on the dead bones of a dragon and watching the procession heading for the graveyard.

'What are you going to do? Before you die?'

Mairi turned her head to look at me. 'When I grow up, do you mean?'

'Yes. No.' And then I was confused. It wasn't just a question about what she'd do, but of what she'd have done by then. 'I mean, if you are just about to die and someone asks you what you've done. What will you say?'

Mairi's mouth pinched up. 'I don't know. How could I know that?'

'I know.'

'Tell us then.'

'Well, I don't know.' And suddenly I didn't know. I was afraid she'd make fun of me, so I forgot.

'What did you say you did for then?'

'Because I did, but now I don't.'

'Whose funeral is it today?'

'James Andrew MacLeman.'

'What did he do?'

'I don't know. He skelped my ear when he caught me picking the brambles at his gate.'

'But they're not his brambles.'

45

'I know. I thought about telling the police on him.'

'You should have.'

'I should have. But the policeman caught me breaking bottles on the shore, so I don't think he'd listen to me.'

I reached over and pulled her collar straight. Her blouse had frilly cuffs and she was leaning on her folded jacket, to keep the blouse clean.

'You're older now.'

She rolled over on her back and held a hand out to me.

'Yes, I am. Come here.'

I moved over beside her. The wind had blown her hair across her face. I moved it aside and leant down to kiss her. The tip of her tongue dabbled lightly at my lips and I let my mind grow empty, letting it fill with sensation: the rock on my knees, the smell of her hair, the warmth and power of her mouth. My hand slipped over her belly, up to her breast – and there was a taste of tobacco smoke and a hint of gin. I pulled back and looked down at her face, the wrinkles round her eyes and her thin lips.

'I'm older now,' she said, and my heart was suddenly painful in my chest.

'Yes. And I am too.' I could feel the breeze playing with the thin hair on the top of my head. I stroked her face gently. My hand was old, the fingers thin. Pale freckles were on the back of my hand. I could almost see the bones and tendons below my skin, I could almost see the cheekbones in her face. Her hair was white.

A car horn sounded, down at the bridge, but when I turned, the road was already empty, a narrow single-track road along the shore, a scattering of houses beside it – and the church standing against the sky and exhorting us all.

I reached down to scratch the itchy place where my shorts always rubbed against my thighs. My mum wouldn't let me get a pair of jeans. Trashy American clothes, she said. But all the other boys wore them – at the weekend, anyway.

'Well, what?' she asked. 'What did you do?'

'I loved you.'

She looked down and picked at the scab on her knee. 'Did

you? Really?'

'Yes.' I turned to look up the valley. The wind was stirring the hazel trees, clouds were moving beyond the hills. When I turned back, her knee was smooth, her dress hung rumpled against her thighs. The top two buttons of her blouse were open, and her eyes were dark and deep and she didn't look shy at all.

'Well? Was that all you did?' She smiled again.

'That wasn't really the kind of thing I was thinking of. But that's what I did with my life.'

'Anything else?'

'Oh yes. I travelled to the other side of the world. I built a house – I mean, really built it, with stones from the field. I spoke to a child that was crying. I don't think he understood me, but he felt better. I found out what I believe about the world – and then I forgot.'

'Nothing big?'

'No. I didn't walk on the moon or win a war. I only did normal things. But they were good things to do – and I wouldn't have done them if I didn't love you.'

Rain spattered on the back of my neck and Mairi was walking away. I thought that I was dying. I felt as if I was, but I knew that people didn't really die of being in love, of being rejected. That was just a way of speaking.

'Mairi!'

She walked away, then began to run, her head shaking.

'Oh god, oh god, oh god!'

I squatted down and wrapped my arms around my knees. The rain soaked through my shirt, running down my back. I grew cold and stiff, but still the tears would not stop. At last I stood up and scrambled down from the rock, falling the last few feet when I stumbled on my untied shoelace. I knelt to tie it up and the setting sun, shining off the loch, dazzled me. I fumbled at the laces, trying to make the bows right, but it was impossible to get them both the same size. I did them as well as I could and stepped down onto the track.

The puddles were quite shallow. I kicked at the water, sending spray up across the sun. After a few puddles I could feel the damp seeping through my socks. I was going to get told off when I got home, but my shoes were wet now anyway. I strode through the next puddle, kicking spray up, first to one side, then the other.

# Parts

From my corner of the classroom I could see my cousin Enrico's seat by the door. He was showing something, a photograph, to the boys on either side of him. His thick black eyebrows waggled suggestively. One of the boys peered at the picture curiously, then suddenly looked shocked. He handed back the photo and faced the teacher as if paying attention, but his eyes were blank.

The teacher turned from the blackboard. 'The skin is an organ.' He said the words firmly, then his mouth clicked shut.

'The basic unit of biology is the cell.' That's what he'd said the very first day in class. He'd articulated the words carefully, letting the short dry sentence emerge from his mouth. Then he waited until we began to write the words down. 'So we will study the cell,' he continued. His face was old and dried out, his mouth could have belonged to a tortoise.

'The basic unit of chemistry is the molecule. We will occasionally refer to it.' It seemed as if the saliva in his mouth had dried out, so that when he spoke he had to pull his lips apart against the tacky residue. He paused again and looked around.

'Classical physics deals with the atom, so we will not.' From the tortoise mouth, sentences emerged. He'd used them so often, they were lifeless: they sat in the air, waiting until we'd all taken note. Then the next one emerged. Once a week we had a double period – nearly two solid hours of biology. Week after week I watched his mouth in horror, unable to ignore it.

'People are cells,' he said. The words meant nothing to me, but he emphasised them as though we should note them.

'Meat is muscle.' I wrote the words down, week after week.

'The kidney is an organ.' Every Tuesday afternoon more raw images of bodily parts emerged from the desiccated mouth.

At dinner time, Enrico was at my table. He was showing the photo again, flushed with excitement, but nervous of getting caught.

Plates rattled at the other end of the canteen. The supervisor turned towards the noise. 'Quiet now!'

While Enrico was watching the supervisor, I reached across and took the photo. It was a Polaroid, bent and creased. All I could see was an ambiguous jumble of black and white. Then I made out a recognisable shape – the pale blob was a girl's face. She had one arm across her eyes. Her other hand was holding something dark. It was her dress. She was holding it right up to her neck. Below, there were white shapes that might be her breasts – so that must be her belly, and there was one of her thighs – most of the picture was still an abstract pattern when Enrico snatched the photo away.

All through the afternoon I held the black and white shapes in my mind, trying to make out what they were.

One of the most annoying things about Enrico staying with us was the way my mother behaved as if he was an adult. She practically simpered at him. As soon as his visit was arranged she did a blitz on the house, touching up the paintwork, replacing the old tablecloth. She even bought a plant for the living room – a Swiss Cheese plant. It had big glossy leaves with holes in them. It looked as if a cat had clawed it while it was growing, so that when the leaves unfolded there were tears in them. I don't know why she bought it. Maybe it's fashionable to have ugly plants in the house.

Enrico was standing in front of the hall mirror again. He'd greased his hair with Brylcreem, and now he was combing it into shiny waves and hollows. It looked like sculpted black lard.

'I read that Michaelangelo once made a lion from butter,' I told him, 'for the centrepiece of a feast.'

'Heh?' He didn't understand, but he saw me grimacing at his hair.

'What wrong with your mouth, little cousin? It look like a hen's arse. You gonna lay a egg, maybe?'

'It looks horrible, Enrico.'

'Hey, when you big enough to chase the girls, you old enough to yap about my hair. Jesus, I bet you ain't even seen a girl's tits, eh?'

I turned away so that he couldn't see me blushing. He laughed and turned back to the mirror.

Later, I was reading in my room. I heard Enrico walking down the hall. He opened the door and threw a magazine at me.

'Look at that, little boy. See what you're missing.' He laughed and shut the door.

The magazine was called *Parade* and there were pictures of women in it. Most of them had hardly any clothes on at all, and there were some pictures in full colour. One of these was in the middle pages, a completely naked woman, lying on a bed. One of her legs was crossed over the other and her hand was on her hip. She was twisted round so that both of her breasts were visible. Her nipples were huge, much bigger than mine.

'James! You haven't done the dishes yet! And have you finished your homework?'

I grabbed the magazine against my chest with the picture hidden, as if she could see through the walls from the downstairs hall.

'I'll come right down, Mum.' I looked frantically round, then stuffed it under the mattress.

Of course she couldn't have known about the magazine. Most of the time she didn't seem to know much about anything at all except keeping the house and cooking. In fact, that was the best way to know what she was thinking.

She still thought I was a child, so she could just walk into my room and tell me to get it tidied up. But she never looked in Enrico's room, and it was much worse than mine. She gave him more food at the table too, like she did for Dad and Grandad. But not for me.

I remember once, when I had just discovered what it was to feel unrequited love. She made a jam steamed pudding because she thought I was looking miserable.

'You must be sickening for something.' she said.

I was furious at her. I could hardly eat the pudding

Compared to biology, physics was a relief. Nothing oozed. Nothing had unpleasant juices. No glistening organs or dissected portions of animals. Instead there were subatomic particles, inelastic collisions, interference patterns and complex lens equations.

Also, the teacher was young and friendly. He explained. He wanted you to understand. He ran a physics club: we built our own radios, and later on, a simple cloud-chamber.

We needed a radioactive source for the chamber. He borrowed my watch.

'The luminous hands have got Radium on them,' he said. 'Watch.'

He put the watch inside and evacuated the glass chamber. We leaned over it, waiting.

'There!'

A tiny white streak of cloud had appeared in the chamber.

'Is that a Radium atom, sir?'

'No, no. Much smaller than that. Even an atom is made of smaller bits. It's mostly empty space with a collection of tiny particles whirling around in it. That was one of them, an electron, leaving its mark as it shot through the chamber.'

So that was it. One of the basic bits that make up everything else. I was silent, thinking about it.

'Of course, even that is probably made of smaller bits,' he said.

Grandad was long-sighted. He had to use a big magnifying glass to read the newspaper, but he could still see well enough to drive.

Every Sunday he'd clean his car and we'd go for a ride, usually out in the country. It was an old car with leather seats. I enjoyed the feeling of being taken somewhere, but I didn't like being out in the country, which is where he always went. It was full of scrappy bushes and old fences that were falling to bits. Half of the houses were empty, or maybe it was just that no-one looked after them. Mostly I looked at the sky while

Grandad told me he was brought up in a place just like this. Wherever we went he'd tell me that. I suppose that was the sort of place he went.

Enrico came with us once, then never again. 'I got better things to do,' he told me, and laughed. After that I was embarrassed to go out with Grandad. Whenever I begged off, he still went, by himself.

The day Enrico left, he gave me his collection of magazines. Most of them were like *Parade*, black and white pictures of women with naked breasts, printed on cheap paper, with just one or two pages of colour photographs on glossy paper.

One of them, though, was different. He must have sent off for it. There was a set of photos of a woman wearing only stockings and a suspender belt. She was standing with her legs apart, staring out at me.

After everyone had gone to bed, I sneaked into the sitting room and took Grandad's big reading glass. I scuttled up to my bedroom, closed the door and turned off the light. Under the blankets, I turned on the torch and opened the magazine. There she was, smiling grimly at the camera, her hands on her hips, her pelvis thrust forwards. I lifted the heavy magnifying glass and held it to the picture, first over her face, then her breasts and then, closer, over the dark place where her legs joined her body.

The illusion of skin and hair broke up into tiny dots. I snorted a laugh. Of course, that was the way printed pictures were made. I moved the lens further away, then closer again. Now you almost see it, now you don't. After a while, it stopped being amusing. I put the reading glass aside, feeling uneasy.

Something moved in the room. I turned off the torch and looked out from under the blankets. The door was still shut, but something unpleasant was moving in the dark. I turned on the torch. The room was empty but the unpleasantness was still there. I could feel it. It was getting worse.

I jumped out of bed and turned on the light. It didn't go away.

I felt the sudden chilly presence of the biology teacher.

53

'People are cells.'

A cold air moved through me. I felt it pass between the cells of my body.

The magazines did not burn well. I crouched over the living-room fire for an hour, stirring the ashes.

At last there was no recognisable piece of ash left. All the lights were on. I was huddled close to the fire.

It hadn't helped.

It was still in the house, somewhere near, waiting. I tried not to think about anything. The wrong thought would bring it close again. I stared straight ahead. There were tiles around the fireplace, cheap bright ones with pictures. From close up, the coloured dots that made up the pictures were clearly visible. I turned away. In the corner of the room, the plant drooped its mutilated leaves. The chill in the room grew worse.

I jumped up and put out the lights, then put coal on the glowing fire and pulled the damper out. In the dimness, the pattern on the tiles was barely visible. I stared at the flames, letting the light drive out thoughts, letting the heat soak in.

Slowly, I warmed up, and fell asleep on the rug.

One Sunday in Spring I went out with Grandad again. Just like before. We came onto some country roads that had been freshly tarred. The road looked like a smooth black ribbon. I sat up and watched it. Among the dreary scraps of hedge and the rusted fences it made such a clean line.

We had a puncture but Grandad didn't mind. He had all the right tools in the boot. He left me to get the spare wheel out while he jacked up the car.

When he'd got the damaged wheel off, I rolled the spare over to him. He had put a pair of overalls on over his Sunday clothes and he was kneeling on the black road. Scraps of tarry grit had stuck to his knee.

I dropped the damaged tyre on the grass verge and sat on it. From inside the car, the edge of the road had seemed to be an exact line. Black tar on one side of the dividing line, grass verge on the other.

Out here, I could see where that tarmac edge was already breaking down, from cars driving close to the edge. Even where there were no car tracks, the road-edge was rough and uneven, if you looked close. There never had been that knife-sharp edge. I'd only imagined it.

In the car on the way home, an unpleasant dizziness twisted inside my head whenever we went round a corner or over a bump. I had to ask Grandad to stop and I was sick. I'd never been car-sick before.

For the rest of the journey, Grandad drove slowly with the windows open. It didn't help much. Acid was burning deep in my throat. The sour taste lined my mouth and I couldn't stop thinking about it as Grandad drove home. All that stuff had been inside me. It had been part of me. When it came up, at what point did the sick stop being me? The thought made me feel worse, but the question wouldn't go away. It roiled with the sick giddiness in my head.

It wasn't just car-sickness. For a week I lay in bed listening to my breath wheezing in and out. In and out.

Mum made jam steamed pudding for me, and brought the plant into my room.

'You need something green in here,' she said. 'Something growing.'

I was too weak to argue. The plant sat near the window with its sad leaves hanging.

I had nothing to do. I couldn't concentrate on a book long enough to read. Most of the time I lay with my eyes shut, but when I opened them, the plant was there.

And one day, when the sun shone in the window, I saw the plant, really saw it, for the first time. Saw why my mother liked it. Each irregular piece of leaf was helping to make a shape. All the bits were working together. I could see the leaf they were trying to make.

That summer my mother let me go down to London to stay with relatives. I'd never been away by myself before. I think she wanted to warn me about city ways, but she just hugged me and said goodbye at the station, and told me to take care.

I was taking the overnight train and managed to get a window seat. I watched the countryside falling away behind us until it was too dark to see out. The train was crowded and hot, but eventually I managed to doze in my seat.

When I woke, it was daylight and we were in the outskirts of town. I reached down my luggage and waited for the station. The rest of the passengers stayed slumped in their seats, dozing. I looked out at the sea of houses and small gardens.

The train showed no signs of stopping and after a while I fell asleep.

When I woke again, the compartment was empty, but the platform outside the window was crowded. I clambered out and stood amongst the bewildering rush of people, looking for the exit. I spotted the barrier, with Aunt Iza standing by it. From far down the platform I heard a voice raised, and then I saw him coming. A crazy man. People made room for him, and he used all the space they gave. Striding confidently down the platform, dirty grey coat flapping and grey hair waving behind him, he looked as if he didn't care about anyone or anything. I tried to avoid his eyes as I made for the exit.

He stopped and pointed at me.

'You!'

I stopped. I couldn't help it. He strode over and stood in front of me.

'In the heart of the atom lives Jesus the Christ!'

Past his shoulder I could see Aunt Iza waving. I tried to step round the man, but I couldn't break away from his intense gaze. I could not get past.

I took one step back. 'No,' I heard myself saying. 'No, I don't think so.'

His eyes lost their fire and he looked puzzled. Then he walked away muttering to himself.

I walked through the barrier and waited for Aunt Iza to kiss me.

She stretched up and pecked my cheek.

'My,' she said, 'haven't you grown!' Then she took my arm and we walked out of the station.

# Jamie's Teeth and the Nature of Reality

Amongst a fairly varied selection of employments, I once spent some time working in an abattoir in Munich. The job was not arduous, as my responsibility was to slip the membraneous tubes onto the dozen or so stainless steel spouts through which was extruded the macerated ends of meat, bones, eyeballs, hooves and suchlike. The tubes, filled with this meatish stuff, were taken on a conveyor belt to the tying station where Donna, an Irish girl, operated the machine that tied them off into fat eight-inch sections.

The place was noisy, but Donna and I managed to develop a wordless relationship during our ten-hour shifts. I was aware of her presence, and I believe that she was aware of mine. When the day was over, and we had removed our rubber boots, ear muffs, eye masks, gloves and overalls, we would sometimes walk back to the hostel together.

This hostel was solely for foreign workers and the common-room was always crowded and noisy with French, Italian and English conversations. Donna and I would talk there sometimes, but she had other friends in the hostel and our relationship was always a possible one, rather than probable.

The rooms in this hostel each had three or four bunk beds, and there was a great deal of indiscriminate visiting in the day-time, when off-shift. Consequently Donna was not surprised when someone came into her room while she was napping. She turned over to look, and saw this person leaving the room. Only later did she find that her silver charm bracelet had gone missing.

We all commiserated with her, and wondered who the thief could have been. I asked if she could recognise the person in her room.

'No,' she replied, 'but I did see that he wore a striped polo-neck sweater.'

Jackie looked at me. 'You've got a striped polo-neck sweater.'

And it was true, I did have such a sweater, but of course I

hadn't stolen the bracelet.

'Give us it back,' said Donna. Her smile was small and uncertain.

I shrugged and smiled back. She wasn't really serious, and nothing further happened. Donna resigned herself to the loss and I ... well, I worried. After all, I could not verify the fact that I hadn't stolen the bracelet. If I had been someone else, I would have suspected me.

That night I lay in my bunk unable to sleep. I could find no memory of stealing the bracelet, but was my lack of memory proof of my innocence?

When I was a child, my father would read Freud's *Psychopathology of Everyday Life* out loud to my mother and me, in the evenings – he did this as he might have read from the Bible, had he still been a religious man. In that book, Freud convincingly described the tricks by which the unconscious leads us to express our repressed desires. It could readily lead me to steal something precious from a young woman that I desired. And, worst of all, it was devious enough to then make me forget what I had done.

At 2 a.m. I got out of bed, careful not to disturb my room-mates, and quietly searched my locker and my bags. I was only slightly relieved to find no bracelet. After all, I might have forgotten where I'd hidden it.

I went back to bed and managed to sleep, eventually.

Unable to prove my innocence to myself, I spent the rest of my stay there in a state of some uneasiness. What particularly upset me was that several other people in the hostel could equally well have been the culprit, but they showed no signs of guilt. There was no trace of worry in their faces.

I have come to understand that there are some people who are completely confident about the nature of the world. They are certain about the events around them. They can specify precisely the words of a conversation some days or weeks in the past, or the disposition of the various vehicles in a minor traffic accident.

I, on the other hand, find that facts are the most nebulous

things, and it is a constant amazement to me that a court of law can pass judgement on even such a simple matter as a petty theft from a newsagent's. To accept only one of many possible interpretations of events! I imagine sometimes what it must be like, to have such a mind. At least, I try to imagine it, and shudder.

Not that criminal incidents are the only events about which I am uneasy. By no means. I am not obsessed with concerns of legality. But such incidents occurring nearby do tend to affect me badly. It is always a relief when any local crime is solved, since I can then be sure that I am not the culprit. For similar reasons, I keep a diary so that I can at least give myself some comfort in the case of the more outstanding of national crimes, by being able to verify my whereabouts at the time in question. Not that there is anything but thin comfort available, as I am well aware that the journal could be a complete fabrication. I find it painfully uncomfortable to remain in any locality where there is a high rate of unsolved crime, and consequently I change jobs often.

I have read a great deal, in bits and pieces: I am not uneducated. I have been advised both by professionals and by well-meaning amateurs. I tend to agree with the suggestions that what they call my problem is due to an incomplete process of primary socialization.

I was an only child in an isolated house, where everything was explained to me, many times. The rules of the house, the way to behave at table, the times when I was allowed to speak, the much longer times when I was required to be silent. One effect of all this was that I never learned to infer the meanings in the behaviour of others. The meaning of an act lay in the rules which allowed it, or compelled it, rather than in any consequence of that act.

Largely this was due to my father, now long gone. I am certain of his role at least, though my mother's acquiescence was perhaps equally important. He was a lapsed minister of the church, and had adopted an idiosyncratic form of logical positivism to fill the gap left when faith departed. If someone threw a towel on the fire, turned the radio on full-blast in the night and scuttled back to bed, or chopped down the cherry tree, as it might be, the evidence logically suggested that I was the culprit. I remember many times, before finally submitting to the authority of his black leather belt, trying to present my version of events. But when it came to proof, my story was always ignored, while circumstantial evidence was given the status of empirical fact: the matches were found in my bed, so I lit the fire. My pleading was always outvoted by my father and my acquiescent mother.

I do recall once committing some forbidden act – by negligence, rather than by bad intention. In something of a panic at the thought of a beating from my father, I carefully prepared the evidence so that it proved that my mother had done the deed. The logical inference of my mother's guilt was completely ignored. I smart still, at the injustice of the punishment I received.

The effect of this childhood training was to lead me to doubt my own testimony, and hence to doubt my memories. I cannot now honestly say that I did *not* perform the other acts for which I was punished. The most that I can say about these long-ago events is that I *may* have been responsible.

However, I have long since come to suspect that my father had a hand in at least some of them.


When my mother was dying, I went to visit her and tried to induce her to talk about these grievances but she was not interested in what I had to say.

'It nearly broke your father's heart,' she said, 'when you cut down the cherry tree.'

'But it's only a figure of speech, mother. We didn't have a cherry tree.'

'No. Not after that.'

'But we didn't ever ...'

She looked at me reproachfully. 'It's just as well your father's gone before. The poor gentle soul would be shocked at you. Telling such fibs to your mother.'

'The poor gentle soul? But he wasn't ...'

'That's enough. I'm tired now,' she said.

'He used to beat me. With his leather...'

'I think I'll have a little sleep,' she said, and closed her eyes. 'You can come and see me tomorrow.'

She died that night.

This is the way it is, for me: I live in a state of constant agony, uncertain of everything, foundering in the meaningless flux of events. The world is like a running stream in which the facts of life are eddies or waves that disappear in a moment. Sometimes I have heard people extolling the virtues of such a viewpoint. 'Going with the flow,' they call it. I can only assume that they are not afflicted with this unfortunate state.

It is difficult to be sociable if you have no sureties in your life, no firm opinions about anything. Consequently, I have an unfortunate tendency to take a stand on the most ridiculously untenable positions, purely for the sake of being, at least temporarily, sure of something. This certainty lasts only as long as it takes for the next person to start speaking. Even if, as has happened more than once, this person agrees with me, I instantly lose any sense of confidence in my own argument.

Is there any reality that we can grasp, that we can wholly rely on? Perhaps this world is a phantasm through which we drift, with no choice and no real ability to act. No-one can be certain. At least, I cannot.

Yet it seems to me that I have caught a glimpse of a process at work that may help me to find a touchstone. In the external world, I cannot verify my experiences by audio or video recording: this would be a cumbersome process and would attract attention. Similarly, soliciting affidavits from witnesses would be considered odd. But I believe that I may have some chance of approaching verification of reality from the other direction, by outwitting the mental processes, by getting in behind them to see what is really there.

Probably it is an everyday event for most of us to censor our memories or to adjust the parameters of memory so that our version of events is more flattering. And there is a similar process at work which enables us to modify our memories to

61

match those of our peers, our friends, our colleagues. There is a great deal of social pressure on us to conform, and this is not limited to dress codes and manner of speech.

A few years back I had a job on a building site with Jamie, a brickie. He used to bring his dog to work, an Irish Springer spaniel. One fine day, sitting in the lee of a shed to eat our lunch, Jamie took his teeth out.

'Watch this,' he said. 'Here, Tash!' he called to his dog.

The spaniel ran over and sat eagerly in front of him. He grabbed her by the head and thrust his false teeth into her mouth. She looked very comical and we both laughed as she threw her head to and fro, until she managed to shake the teeth back out.

Still grinning, Jamie picked up the teeth, wiped them cursorily on his coat sleeve and put them back in his mouth.

Astonished as I was, I said nothing. Though I tend to find people's thoughts and motivations difficult to divine, I have gathered that there is a certain social finesse about such matters, which varies with occupations. I had not worked in the building trade before. Perhaps among brickies and masons, this somewhat unhygienic behaviour was considered normal.

I ran into Jamie from time to time, after the job had finished, and I met him in a bar a couple of years later, to celebrate his engagement. During the evening, various acquaintances told tales of his terrible past, as the way is, to embarrass him in front of his fiancée. I took the opportunity to join in.

'Do you mind the time you put your false teeth in the dog's mouth? On that job over at Gairloch?'

'I never did! You're making it up!'

And in that moment it happened and I saw it. In the face of his obvious desire not to be associated with the act which I remembered, I let the matter drop. But also, mirroring this adjustment in social reality, I perceived, fast as a wink, a matching adjustment in my own internal reality. Somewhere between two thoughts, a switch flopped, a gate closed, and what had been a sure and certain memory was suddenly fogged and dim. An adjustment had been made in the status of the memory.

So now I know how he works, the villain of the piece. If I didn't exactly see his hand at work, I saw the shadow of it.

I'm waiting now, and next time there is a sudden deletion or an adjustment of memory, I'll be in there like a shot, in behind the thoughts and false memories to where reality is.

# Many Legs

The millipede has not got a thousand legs. The centipede has far less than a hundred. Only when we move further down the scale of leggy multiplicity do we find that popular belief is close to accurate. While the squid has most people baffled, it is both widely and correctly believed that the octopus has eight legs. And insects have six. Though here there is room for discussion, if not outright contention: an insect's antennae are modified legs and even its mandibles are legs that have developed into strange but useful forms. We have all seen a close-up shot of an ant or a beetle eating: it is using different motions, different actions, even different organs from those that we use for the task. Some of us find this oddness deeply disturbing.

Among humans, our legs rarely have anything to do with our eating practices, though it has to be said that in cases of enforced cannibalism – and presumably also in elective cannibalism – the leg is a prized portion, being fine and fleshy. And most of us find this disturbing also.

An acquaintance of mine once felt compelled to show me a very old encyclopaedia that he had obtained in an auction. In this book was a monochrome photograph of a Russian commissar sitting by a stout man with a thick peasant face. They were on a bench outside; the ground was white with snow and they both wore clothes of fur. The commissar looked a little smarter but he wore his hat at an odd angle as if he was, if not drunk, then at least a little tipsy.

I could see little of note in the picture, until I read the caption. It appeared that in times of famine, the stout man sold human flesh to the people of the area. It was a family tradition. No-one else sold human meat, just this man and his family. For several generations, they had occupied, and indeed defended, this economic niche. There was no suggestion that they killed people. Their trade was an opportunistic one: they were scavengers rather than predators. Though it appeared from the text that, in a bad year, it was a full-time occupation.

The commissar, who had evidently set up the photographic session, did not look afraid or even worried, to be sitting next to a purveyor of human meat. This was as disquieting as anything else – that this official seemed to find the situation a bit of a lark, rather than deplorable. He might even carry a copy of the photo around in his wallet, to show to strangers in bars.

'Look, this is me, and this is the cannibal butcher of Rodinsk!'

Looking more closely at the picture, the background details became clearer. What appeared to be a pile of old clothes was, in fact, a human body, still clothed, lying on a heavy table. A leg was lying on the icy ground, in a macabre visual pun, beside the table leg. Other bits and several whole bodies were stacked against the wooden wall behind.

The picture was fascinating, though I suppose that it was my response that was most interesting. When I first looked at the picture, I saw two men, quite normal-looking, though in an old-fashioned way. After I read the caption and saw the bodies in the background, their faces changed, grew sinister.

Pictures of mass-murderers, politicians, habitual mis-users of the possessive apostrophe and other similar human renegades, rarely show anything unusual. I might look at a photo in the newspapers and think that this person looks like any everyday person you might meet on the street. Then I read what the person did or is accused of, and the relaxed smile becomes a ruthless sneer. The calm gaze becomes the blank stare of a psychopath. That is understandable, of course. We project our thoughts and emotions onto other people. Given a set of photos of perfectly normal people mixed in with these criminals, I could not pick out any essential difference. On the visual evidence alone, these people are normal. And that is worrying. Could I be living next door to a mass-murderer? A cannibal? Conversely, the man across the road, who wears a neatly trimmed brown moustache and carries a meat cleaver in his belt – is he, in fact, perfectly normal?

When I was of an impressionable age, I read an essay of George Orwell's. In the course of his essay, Orwell claimed that food rarely looks like food, though he does give just one counter-example. He comments on a species of antelope, saying that it was impossible to look at the hindquarters of the beast without thinking of mint sauce. The rest of his essay is lost to me, though I think it was about the use of words.

If we can project our emotions on to newspaper pictures of violent and degraded people, then plainly we can do the same for foods. I suspect that Orwell was not a gustatorily oriented person. Or perhaps he was rarely hungry. I have been hungry and I can tell you that a young cauliflower is an unalloyed delight, and on occasion I have nearly wept over a carrot.

To be fair to Orwell, I think he was referring specifically to animals. Yet even here, it seems to me that he betrays a lack of culinary imagination. I have experimented over the years, discovering that while it may have been true for Mr Orwell, it is by no means so for me. It is true that a dog, no matter how hard I try to imagine it, cannot look like food. Even the American hot dog does not look like food to me. Similarly with the cat. I think it is the hairiness that puts me off.

Cows rarely look like food – but I once met a water buffalo in India that seemed to invite the carving knife. It looked at me with its beautiful brown eyes and let me pat its shoulder. I had even been introduced to it and to its owner, but I could not help thinking what a fine meal it would make. Pigs too, especially the piglets, look very toothsome. It may well be that other people find the sheep a delectable mammal, but I do not. A lamb, perhaps, but not a full-grown sheep. I'm sure that there are personal preferences in these things.

Orwell's assertion remained with me, however. I was annoyed that I couldn't argue it out with him. Now and then I would check it out once more: yes, that mackerel still says, 'Eat me;' that rabbit is crying out to be served in a thick gravy with bay-leaves. And then I would tell myself, 'See? He was wrong.'

I encountered a girl called Jill. She had long dark henna-ed hair and wore hippie skirts and a wonderful scent with a hint of citrus and vanilla. I was nervous of approaching her directly, but eventually, without too much engineering on my part, I found myself sharing a drink with her and several of our mutual friends. I was delighted to find that she noticed and seemed to reciprocate my interest. We chattered about nothing in particular and laughed at things that were not funny. Eyes looked into eyes – it was going pretty well. Then she had to visit the toilet, and as she slid out from the banquette seat, her skirt rode up and I saw her leg right up to her solid thigh. My heart gave a little leap and she smiled at me as I blushed and turned my head away.

I sat there, aware that I was a little drunk and might be misreading the situation. 'She was just embarrassed,' I told myself – but her smile had definitely held more than that. The brief flash of thigh drifted into my mind's eye – and as will happen to a lovesick person, it acquired all sorts of alluring properties. I could feel myself melting. But I knew exactly what happened when I let myself melt. I became incapable of conversing rationally and I lost all practical ability to perform everyday actions like standing up without knocking over a chair or opening a door courteously without looking and feeling like a fool.

So I carefully, in a mature and sensible way, looked at my reaction to her thigh. It's just a thigh, I thought. Be sensible. What effect can a thigh have on you? You've got two of them, everyone has. The vision of her thigh drifted up in front of me, desire arose and before I could stop it, George Orwell's little throwaway comment drifted into my mind. Jill's thigh suddenly looked like the most wonderful food. I laughed the thought away. Amazing what the mind could do.

Jill returned and sat closer to me than before, so that her leg was touching mine. In a few short minutes, time was called and we all drifted out into the street. Jill and I dragged our feet, letting everyone walk further and further ahead of us. They all turned the corner and Jill took my hand and pulled me into a doorway. In a moment our lips were pressed against each other, mouths opening as we urgently tried to press them still closer.

When the thought arrived, I stopped moving completely, then shuddered. Jill held herself against me for a moment longer, then pulled away and looked up.

'You all right?'

'Yes. Sorry. I've got to get home.'

'What? What's wrong?'

'George Orwell,' I said. 'And the mandibles of insects.'

'Insects!'

'Not just insects,' I said, unhappily. 'Segmented beasts in general.'

I think, if people still did such things, she would have slapped my face. And I wouldn't have blamed her. In fact, it might have made me feel a bit better. Instead, she kicked me in the knee. It was very painful, and my leg collapsed.

I looked up at her, glaring down at me. 'Your legs are beautiful,' I said. And indeed they were – tall and solid legs that were both sensual and muscular. I lay there, my heart aching as I listened to her shoes clacking away up the street. She left behind her a sweet scent of citrus and vanilla.

# The Perfect Loaf

# The Perfect Loaf

The young man has a battered book propped open on the kitchen table. The book has flecks of bread dough stuck on the cover. The dough is old and brittle; it could easily be removed. He likes it the way it is.

There is a big plastic bowl beside the book. He fetches flour and sugar from the cupboard, yeast from the fridge. He blows old flour from the pages and bends to read the book.

*Take three or four cups of lukewarm water.*

Faraway in the past, an old man, a floury dwarf, puts the last tray into the Scotch oven and shuts the cast iron door.

The boy's father is ill, and his grandfather is helping out.

'I'm just off up to the house to see how your father is. Mind the bakery for me.'

'All right, Grandpa.'

As soon as the door shuts, the boy fetches a chair and climbs up to get the icing sugar from the cupboard. He drags a box over to the huge wooden work table and takes the saucepan that stands beside the single gas-ring which is always kept lit.

He takes the saucepan to the tap, half-fills it, and climbs on the box again.

'When you're making water icing, the water has to boil. That's the secret of it.'

That's what his grandpa had said. So now the boy knows the secret.

He stands by the table, waiting for the water to boil. It seems to take far too long. If he is caught playing with the gas-ring he'll be in trouble – but if he has a saucepan full of perfect icing, well that would be different.

He jitters nervously, from the table to the door and back, to check if his grandfather is returning.

At last he can stand it no longer. He spoons in the icing sugar and stirs. Almost instantly, he has a saucepan half full of runny icing with lumps in it. He stirs desperately, trying to mash the lumps down into a smooth paste. It doesn't work. He adds some more water, then more icing sugar to thicken it up...

When he hears his grandfather returning, he abandons the saucepan in panic and stands by the steam-press, trying to look as if it has nothing to do with him.

Grandpa spots the saucepan immediately. He looks into it and grunts.

'Hmmph.'

He takes the saucepan to the deep sink and drops it in the water. Nothing more is said.

> *Mix in half an ounce of baker's yeast and two ounces of sugar. Put the creamed yeast in a warm place for a few minutes.*

The young man takes the jug to the shelf above the gas cooker. There is no room there, so he lifts off a small pile of paperbacks and puts the jug in the empty space.

He looks around the room. Apart from the table, where he is about to make bread, there is no surface left that is not covered by kitchen utensils or more books. He gathers several notebooks together, stacks them upright and squeezes the paperbacks into the space.

He returns to the battered recipe book.

> *Take one pound of wheat flour and a teaspoon of salt, mixed lightly into the warmed flour.*

In the dim bakery, the sun shines in slants through the dusty windows. Thick with flour motes, the sun beams fall on the grey concrete floor and the edge of the massive pine work table. From low down, where he is playing with a piece of dough, the boy cannot see the table top, but the smell of candied peel, sugar and flour drifts down, mixing with the scent of warm rolls rising in the steam-press.

The flour seems to settle out of the air onto the old man.

His white hair and eyebrows are furred with it; his shirt and his trousers are almost as white as the old flour-sack he uses for an apron. Compared to the other two bakers, he is small, but he is magical in his smallness, like a dwarf, or one of the small dark Picts who used to inhabit our land.

Though the old man is only helping out for a few days, the other bakers defer to him, subtly, in the way they work. The elder of these is the old man's son, and the owner of the bakery. The boy does not usually see his father like this, waiting to let someone else speak first, and occasionally hesitant in his actions, as if waiting to be corrected. There is less talk too, when the old man is there. A small part of the awareness of each man is watching him, seeing the easy movements, the economy of action that he has learnt in over sixty years of baking.

*The yeast should be frothing by now.*

Sundays were different when the old man came up to stay. The boy's family never went to church, but as the old man was a Kirk elder, he dressed in a dark suit and went to the Kirk three times. There was an uncomfortable quiet about the house, and the children played up on the moors to be out of the way.

Somehow, on Sundays, the old man seemed more than old. He was ancient, and his age could hardly be measured in years.

Sometimes his father talked to the boy about his grand-father. It was like hearing an ancient myth, for the old man's life spanned epochs. Historical events punctuated his life. He was already a time-served baker when the Boer War was being fought, and by the time of the Great War he had a bakery of his own. By the end of the Thirties, he had three bakeries.

After the Clydebank Blitz he had one left. His family were grown by then, and he was happy to run just that one for a few years before retiring.

*Pour two tablespoons of oil and the creamed yeast into the middle of the flour.*

Bubbles rise and burst slowly. The heady smell fills the kitchen. The young man takes the jug to the table. He pours the liquid into the flour, where it gathers in a hollow.

*Mix well until the mixture begins to cling together.*

The old man, being an elder of the Kirk, did not drink alcohol. But when he was visiting his son's family he would make his own ginger beer. A big bowl, with yeast, sugar, warm water, ginger and a couple of lemons chopped in. The bowl was put in the cupboard beside the sink in the bakery – the only cupboard with a key. The boy never got the chance to try the ginger beer, but he could smell it: in the cupboard, bubbles rose and burst. The smell drifted through the bakery.

*A pinch of ginger may be added at this stage, if desired.*

The boy sits under one end of the table while the bakers have their tea. The old man is telling a story.

'I was working at John Munro's bakery at the time – this was before the First War – and in those days we didn't have yeast. We used barm. It was a kind of beer, and we made it in troughs in the bakery.

'Well, one winter morning, a couple of scaffies came in for a heat. The bakers were at work on the big table top, pounding and mixing a mass of dough. The lids were off the barm troughs, and on such a bitter cold morning, of course one of the bakers offered the scaffies a mug of barm. And of course if the scaffies had a mugful, then the bakers, since their master had gone upstairs, had to have a mugful too.'

The boy played quietly out of sight, listening.

'Well, one mug led to another, and in the warm atmosphere of the bakehouse, with the oven lit and waiting for the bread, it wasn't long before they all became drowsy and fell asleep. And the dough on the table was forgotten.

'An hour or so later, one of the scaffies woke his mate. Each as befuddled as the other, they leaned on the table for support, and saw there the heap of dough which the bakers had abandoned. It had been growing while they slept, and it was about to overflow onto the floor. The bakers were in no state to deal with it, so the scaffies decided to help.

'Somehow, still drunk as they were, they managed to heave the dough in armfuls off the table and over to the oven. They stuffed the lot in, then closed the oven door and left.

'The bakers slept on, and in the oven, the dough began to heat up. The outside grew crusty and brown, while on the inside the barm continued to work, and the dough swelled up and began to push the oven door open. Before long, the oven doorway was filled with a large rounded mass of crusty brown bread.

'It was just then that the master baker's wife came downstairs on an errand. She took one look round the bakery, then turned and ran back up the stairs, screaming, "John, John! Come quickly! The bakers are all deid and there's a horse in the oven!" '

*Turn the dough out onto a floured surface.*

The old man had three sons and one daughter. He talked to his grandson about them while they worked together in the bakery. One son was a doctor, in Glasgow. Another was a lecturer at the college. The daughter was headmistress of a secondary school.

'They've all done well,' he said.

'What about my dad?' the boy asked.

'Aye, he's done well too. Maybe he's done best of all.'

*Knead well, and set the dough in a warm place to rise.*

The young man sets the mixing bowl on top of the cooker and sits at the table with a book. Sadness can creep in at this point in the process. He has to wait on the yeast to do its stuff, and the empty time is filled with the ghost of his grandfather, silent and invisible, but certainly present.

There had been a falling out between the old man and his son. It was summertime, and the old man had come up from Clydebank to help out in the busy season. The boy had grown, and was helping where he could, picking up and storing tips from his grandfather. 'You have to make fondant on a marble slab, and keep working it while it cools. If you don't, you just end up with a big lump of sugar.'

Then the old man was told that his son had decided to give up the bakery. The trade was too uncertain, too seasonal, and the big bakeries were sending trucks up the West twice a week, supplying the local shops. The father would go to teacher training college. The family were to move to the East Coast so that he'd be able to get home at weekends.

The old man listened silently, and when his son paused for comment, he just said, 'It's your decision.'

Then the old man turned back to his work. The boy was watching, and saw something too terrible to be borne. The magic drained out of his grandfather. The floury dwarf was gone, and there was just an old man filling pie cases. The boy turned and ran from the bakehouse.

*When the dough has doubled in size, turn it out onto a board and knead lightly.*

At the age of eighty-five, the old man stepped off a bus, as it slowed for a corner. This was to avoid walking a hundred yards from the bus-stop to his front door. He'd done it all his life.

The boy's father was a teacher by now. He took time off and went to sit with the old man while he died.

*Put the dough into oiled tins and set them to rise for a further twenty minutes.*

The boy was in a strange way pleased: not at his grandfather's death, but at the manner of his going. There was spirit in that, at eighty-five, jumping off a moving bus.

His father stayed in Clydebank a few days more, to settle

affairs. When he returned, the boy did not know what to say, what to ask. His father told him anyway.

'He was clear in his mind right to the end.' The boy nodded, said nothing.

'We didn't talk much, but he did say one thing. A regret he had.' The boy looked up.

'He told me that there were so many beautiful words, and he'd never had the chance to use them.' The boy and his father looked at each other.

'I think he wanted me to tell you. He said it twice, so it was important.'

*Bake in an oven at 375°F for 45 minutes.*

Now the boy is grown, and here he sits at the kitchen table in his flat. Reading. The room is full of the smell of bread baking.

# Reading the Signs

I could feel the sudden exhaustion coming on, the draining of energy. The hallmark of hepatitis. Though the sun was down, the heat was still intolerable. The crowds surged around me, noise and smell and constant jostling. The street was long.

I made it into the shelter of a broad doorway, and slumped against the wall. This doorway was familiar by now: the entrance to one of the dozens of clothes emporia on this street, with gaudy signs crying out – Best Quality Silk – Goods Prepared for Export – with smaller script in Hindi underneath, repeating the message. But I had no interest in the clothes.

The doorway was wide and deep, with room for a weighing machine at this side and at the other side a young Sikh with a trolley, selling soft drinks. I looked at the weighing machine. I knew I couldn't really afford it, but I gave in to curiosity.

Rummaging in the pockets of my light cotton trousers, I found a small coin, twenty paese. I stood on the weighing machine, pushed the coin into the slot. There was a short pause, then the machine extruded a purple ticket. I read it.

**– Weight 118.5 pounds. Ideal height
for this weight: 5′ 7″ –**

I gazed at the ticket, letting my brain cope with the information as fast as it could. The exhaustion of hepatitis had receded. The weakness that remained was due solely to the heat and the humidity. And dysentery. And too little food. And too much hashish – though that had mostly stopped when the illness began.

I shrugged it off. The list could go on and on. Right now what I needed to concentrate on was the medically-proven fact – I punctuated the reasoning process by waving the confirming ticket – that I needed to lose four inches in height in order to match my weight. Last week, I was only two inches too tall.

Of course there might be money waiting for me at the International Telephone Exchange, telegrammed from home.

In that case, I could get a plane ticket and then start to deal with my problem from the other direction – by gaining weight. At the moment, the only available foods that I and my stomach could agree on were chicken soup, white bread rolls and Madeira cake.

I fantasised for a few moments about the flight home. The cool interior, that inoffensively bland music they always play ... I could see the stewardess bringing me an airline meal on a sterile plastic tray: I would ask for another one, even a third ... the stewardess would be unable to resist my famished look, the appeal in my dark, sunken eyes.

I sighed as I stepped off the platform. I waited for a break in the flow of people going in and out, then crossed the doorway to the soft-drink stall.

'One Limca, please, cold.'

The bottle came out of the icebox, and was opened with a slight frigid hiss. I handed over a couple of rupees and gratefully sipped, leaning against the warm wall. In my other hand I still had the ticket from the weighing machine. I held it up to read the motto printed on it. The print was fuzzy from my sweat, but still readable.

> – It is nice to be important, but it is
> more important to be nice. –

I threw it away in disgust. I felt cheated. I'd seen that one already, on a sign in the bus station in Jammu.

There were signs like that in all public places – railway stations, post offices, police stations – all of them more or less insipid homilies exhorting the public to moderate behaviour. Presumably this was to dissuade the public from leaping over the counter and throttling the dilatory, thoughtless, petty-minded, unhelpful, arrogant employees who had obtained their posts by nepotism or bribery, and cared nothing about the members of the public who depended on their services. This preventative propaganda was wasted on me. I was fit neither to leap counters nor to throttle.

These notices were impossible to ignore, but since I'd fallen

ill, I had learnt to view their awful smugness with some detach-
ment. It wasn't worth getting upset. Any flash of anger, or even
annoyance, was followed within seconds by an overwhelming
reaction: almost complete limpness, too weak to do anything
but rest and wait for strength to return.

I had allowed myself a full hour to cover the few hundred
yards to the Telephone Exchange, hoping to leave myself an
hour to deal with the counter staff. Despite my illness and the
heat, I made the journey every morning as well as the evening.
I had heard harrowing tales of what happened to money orders
if the intended recipient did not get there soon enough. The
cash got siphoned off into a high-interest account somewhere,
and once it had disappeared, it would not reappear for three
months or more. Long before three months, my ideal height
would have diminished to zero.

At last, with many stops in helpful doorways, I reached
the place. Gratefully, I pushed into the dim cool interior, my
sandals hushing on the marble slabs of the floor. As the doors
swung shut behind me, the roar of traffic and crowds subsided.
I stood quite still for a moment, absorbing the coolness and
the relative quiet. I took a string of beads from my pocket
and began chanting a mantra silently to myself. Then I joined
a queue. I knew the score by now. If you joined the shortest
queue, the man at the front of your line had to telephone to
some obscure place in Turkey, where the phone system was even
worse than here. If you had to choose between two identical
queues, the counter closed just as you reached it. There was
no winning strategy. Best just to choose a line at random, and
accept that the die was cast.

It was 7.30pm by the time I reached the counter, and by
then I had recited my mantra all the way round the rosary
and back 100 times, and had read my way through all the
uplifting messages hung on the walls to indoctrinate the irritable
customer. There was a sign on the counter too, saying – Please
check your balance before leaving the counter – I'd read it, and
agreed with it, dozens of times, when I finally got the chance
to ask my one simple question:

'Is there a telegram for MacKay?'

'No. Nothing.'

I sat on one of the seats by the wall and looked around. The chai-wallah was at the far end, serving customers. I caught his eye and signalled. He acknowledged me with a smile, then went into a small side-room. When he came out, there was a slice of cake on his tray along with the teapot and glasses.

'Good evening, sahib. Chai?'

'Chai, thank you.' He poured tea into a glass, handed it to me. 'Do you have any cake today?'

'Yes, sahib, I have it here.' He handed it over with a flourish.

This was a ritual we'd developed over the last few days. The first time I'd come to the Exchange, it had been early in the day, and the place had been nearly empty. When I asked for cake with my tea, he insisted that of course he had some, then ran off to a shop to buy me a slice. When he learned that I was waiting for money, he told me that he would buy a whole cake.

'Waiting for money takes time, sahib. But I will buy a small cake, not a large one. With good fortune, the money will come before the cake is finished.'

Today, the slice of cake had a piece of paper stuck to the end. I peeled it off. I looked up at the chai-wallah.

'Is it finished?'

'Acha. It is the last piece.'

I sighed and passed him a half-rupee.

'Dhaniovad,' he said. 'Thank you.' He lingered for a moment. 'Perhaps tomorrow, sahib.'

As the time approached 7.45pm, I decided to try again. The hall seemed unpleasantly cold now, and I shivered as I stood up.

The walk across the floor was difficult: sitting in the cold had stiffened my muscles and the short walk had me breathing heavily, head swimming. I was in luck, though. There was a short queue, with only two people, and by squeezing in close, no matter what the man in front thought, I was able to get one hand on the counter for support. There I stood, head hanging, breathing slowly, until my time came. I could barely lift my head to speak.

'MacKay? Anything?'

The man didn't even check the pigeonholes.

'Nothing.'

I knew I should insist that he check, but I had had enough. I turned, knocking the sign to the floor. I stopped, swaying, then carefully bent down and tried to pick it up. Blackness began rising around me, I could feel myself swaying, knew I was about to faint. 'This is it ... this is what it's like ... I hope I relax enough ... that marble is hard.'

Someone gripped my arm, helped me to a chair. I slumped down, the blackness still surging around me, but slowly subsiding.

The hand left my arm and a cup was pushed into my hand.

'Pani ... Water, sahib.' It was the chai-wallah.

I drank, began to recover.

'Thank you ...' I could manage nothing more, just sat back, breathing slowly and carefully.

I shook my head ruefully. It was time to go. This place shut in another ten minutes. I looked sadly up at the pigeon-holes behind the counter.

The chai-wallah was walking along the counter now, offering tea to those few left in the queues. As he bent to pick up the sign that I had knocked down, he looked over at me and waved to get my attention. I looked back, puzzled. He put the sign back in its place, then tapped the counter in front of it, looking significantly at me.

At last I read the sign and made the connection – *Please check your balance before leaving the counter* – I grinned and nodded at him, and he wandered away, satisfied.

I shook my head over the joke, smiling to myself. Who would have guessed that the chai-wallah could read English? But I had come across odd tales of highly accomplished people taking on menial work – something to do with the Hindu religion, a kind of salvation by good works – karma yoga – that was it. Well, he'd certainly done his good deed for today. There were other stories, too, about highly-developed human beings who moved among ordinary people incognito, helping them. Some kind of Hidden Order. And, in this day and age, where better to be situated than here, in the nerve centre of the Indian telecommunications network? And what a strange thing that was, if you stopped to think of it, the electromagnetic pulses travelling outward through the earth's atmosphere, people at the other end of the world acting on the merest breath of electrical discharge from this, the External Nervous System of the Planet...

The immediate surroundings seemed to fade away, and I found myself, from some vastly high vantage point, looking down at the planet, seeing its aura of life laid over the delicate blue and white. I could see the shimmer of radio waves and I could see a shining web of light, and I knew that it was the global telephone network. I could see electromagnetic waves travelling outwards from Earth, growing fainter, but never disappearing completely.

I looked down at the planet, and my viewpoint began to move, down through the electromagnetic shimmer, details appearing then passing by as I went down towards the blue-white globe. Faster now, over the parched lands of India, rushing vertiginously into the turmoil of Delhi, and down into a low building where, with a sickening lurch, I found myself once more in my sick body in a chilly hall.

The chai-wallah was at the counter again. He was frowning this time, and pointing more vehemently than before. I separated myself from my drifting thoughts. This time I understood right away. This Illuminated Man had seen the turmoil of my thoughts, and was urging me once again to keep my balance. He was right, of course. I nodded to him, and held up my thumb, to show that I understood and agreed. He looked at me dubiously, before going about his tasks.

Quite right, I was thinking to myself, this is no time to let my thoughts get out of control. I'm in a bad way, and my job just now is to take care of myself as best I can. It was very sharp of him to notice that I was drifting away. How did he notice? Well, I suppose a highly developed individual like him might notice something from muscle tone and posture, things like that. But no. Don't worry about it. Keep balance. Quiet.

'Sahib!'

'What?' I woke up.

'Sahib,' he hissed, leaning over me. 'There is a letter. Maybe for you.'

'What?'

'Under the counter. There is a letter. He put it there.'

'A letter?'

'Shhh!' he hissed, then 'Chai, sahib?' in a loud voice.

'Where?'

'Under the counter, by the sign.'

And suddenly it all became clear. His cryptic messages had merely been crossed wires. He could not read. He was not an Illuminated Being at all. He was something much more important. A friendly and helpful person.

I slipped him a rupee as I stood and slowly made my way back to the counter.

'I believe there is a telegram for me.'

'Nothing for MacKay.'

'Will you check, please?'

'There is nothing.'

With a bite in my voice, I spoke louder. 'Will you please check?'

The man opened his mouth, but before he could speak, I put in, 'I insist!'

'Very well.'

As the man turned and walked over to the pigeon holes, I lifted myself up and leaned over the counter as far as I could. There was something there, an envelope, but I couldn't see the name. I dropped to the floor again, panting.

'As I said, nothing. I am sorry. Perhaps tomorrow.'

Anger flared.

'Now listen to me!' I shouted.

The man stepped back in shock and I reeled as my vision blurred. I didn't know what to say next. I was sure it was my telegram there under the counter and I was desperate to get it. My voice dropped to a lower level, but clear and menacing.

'I received a phone call this morning from my bank. They

assured me that the money had been sent, and would be here by this evening. If you can't help, then I insist on seeing the supervisor.'

'Sir, there is nothing...'

'The supervisor! I want the supervisor! I will not move from this place until I have my telegram!' I stopped bellowing, feeling that I could last longer with the low and menacing voice. 'And if I do not get satisfaction, I will have the ambassador and the police in here to turn over the whole festering bunch of you!'

My voice had become a bellow again, and I took hold of the counter with both hands, for support while I recovered.

When I managed to raise my head again, there was another man there, in an expensive suit, having a whispered consultation with the counter clerk. The supervisor came over, rubbing his hands together in distress.

'I am most terribly sorry, sir, that this should occur. These counter clerks,' he gestured dismissively along the counter, 'they are so inefficient. Mr. Colaco,' he paused slightly, and the clerk winced, knowing that he was to be the scapegoat, 'he says that there may have been a small mix-up when the shift was changing.'

'Well? Where is it?'

'We will do our best, sir...'

'I want it now!' I reeled and grasped the edge of the counter, head bent. To someone who did not know I was ill, it must have appeared that I was barely containing a homicidal frenzy.

'Oh, sir! Here it is!' With a lightly forced laugh, the supervisor pulled the envelope from under the counter. 'Mr. Colaco must have misplaced it!'

As the supervisor passed it over, my hand fell heavily onto it.

'This contains a money order. You will cash it for me.'

'I regret, sir, it is past eight...'

That was it. My response was wholly irrational, but consequences no longer mattered. I felt that I would willingly cripple myself for life, suffer brain damage and face charges of breach of the peace. Anything, but I would get my money out of these...

'Aaahhh!' I had their attention. 'I have had enough! You will pay me the money! I am telling you so!'

Before the echoes had gone, the clerk was counting out money in piles of one thousand rupees apiece, while the supervisor was apologising and berating Mr. Colaco. I stood and watched, saying nothing.

At last the money was counted. The supervisor pushed Mr. Colaco out of the way and handed over the notes with a beaming smile.

'Always glad to be of service. Sorry about the small problem...'

I was shivering violently from reaction and the chill of the place. I scooped the money into my bag, gathered myself together and managed to stride across the hall and out of the doors before collapsing to the ground for a rest.

Back at the hotel I spent a wonderful evening just lying on my bed, dreaming about home. I wasn't even very upset when I found that Mr. Colaco, probably more out of habit than cupidity, had short-changed me by 200 rupees.

# Scrimshaw

It isn't easy, conjuring a bone up out of the ground. But I have done it, with only three young people, a dog and a small landslide.

There we are, on a Spring day in an old graveyard, surrounded by old trees. The dog is gambolling around the bushes, hoping for rabbits. One girl is picking daffodils, one is swinging on the curved branch of a cedar. I am watching them all, the mad energy of the dog, the quietness of Anna, picking flowers. My younger sister, Margaret, in the tree, swinging and singing to herself.

'I'm going in there,' I declare, and I head off down an earthen ramp between brick walls. It leads along a passage to the vault of the local laird's family. As I move along the passage, the light grows less, until I can barely make out the empty sandstone doorway that leads into the vault. The doors have fallen in long ago.

Behind me, the girls have come to watch, holding arms for comfort.

I step into the vault and the soft hummocky sand underfoot feels just like the darkness pressing against my face, undefined and threatening.

Two steps I go, then another. Then I turn around, and I cannot see the doorway. I can't see anything. In a moment of panic, I lose my sense of where I am and where the door might be. My heart is pounding.

Then I hear the girls whispering in the passageway. I still can't see the doorway, but I know roughly where it is. I close my eyes and that is better. Now I don't expect to see anything, so the dark is easier to cope with.

My heartbeat slows, though it is still fast.

'Come out, Alan.' It is Margaret.

'Please.' Anna.

'Nay,' I boom back. 'Never shall I leave this dire and dreadful place!'

The sound of my own voice frightens me again and I shuffle

forwards, arms out, towards the door. My fingers touch
sandstone, then I find a gap. I step forward again and there is
a scent of daffodils, then Anna's hand is on my arm and I can
see the walls.

The girls stay close, reaching out to pat me now and then
as we walk up the ramp and into the bright, green graveyard,
where light touches everything. There is sound, too. Birds are
calling, the dog is scrambling around the undergrowth outside
the fence. Where the hillside has slipped, several metal posts
are hanging free, and Merlin has scrambled underneath and
is rooting about in the gully beyond.

'Merlin! Here, boy!'

There is a brief pause before the dog's head pokes under
the fence. In his grinning jaws there is a stick.

'Here, boy! Good dog!'

The dog struggles through and gallops up to us.

'It's a bone! That's not a stick, it's a bone!'

It's true. Though it looks like a thumb-thick stick, it has two
unmistakeable bulges, one at each end to fit into a shoulder
or an elbow joint.

Anna steps back, hugging her bunch of daffodils. Her eyes
are wide.

Margaret laughs. 'Where did you get that, you stupid
dog?'

'Get it off him!' Anna's voice is high.

'Drop it. Drop it!'

I hold the dog by the collar and Margaret prises the bone
from his jaws.

'Got it!' She holds it up high and Merlin leaps. Birds are
calling in the ivy, up in the trees. Wind is whispering through
the bare branches of elm, through the evergreen cedar.

Margaret holds the bone high and Merlin leaps for it.
Margaret is laughing, Anna is fearful.

I am watching.

Margaret looked after the bone for the next few years. It
usually stayed in her room, but it was often found in other
parts of the house.

In the living room, my father would pick it up and idly tap it on his glass ashtray, keeping time to the music for *Going for a Song* or *The Beiderbecke Tapes*.

I believe, though I have no proof, that for Margaret it was the prime agent in a ritual designed to make various young men of the village fall in love with her. It seemed to work. Possibly she also used it to put a hex on her rivals – but there was less direct evidence of that.

For my part, I used to stand on one leg and point the bone backwards over my shoulder, aiming its influence at imaginary enemies. Sometimes I did this in the garden, where everyone could see. It didn't work.

Anna never really took to the bone, or said she didn't. But I think she really rather enjoyed the frisson of the macabre that surrounded the bone – or the idea of having it in the house.

Mum looked at it from time to time and frowned, wondering why she didn't find this strange object an unpleasant intruder, why she didn't insist on its being removed from the house. Then she'd turn back to the TV with a little shrug, and the bone would stay.

If the bone had any energy clinging to it, it was not malevolent. I liked to think that the bone was enjoying this little excursion, before it got back to its job of mouldering away.

The bone is in the house now, though it took some ingenuity to get it there. My grandfather, on the other hand, is no problem. There he sits, where he always sits, in his small house near the beach. His tools are laid out on a cloth on the coffee table, and he works away for hour after hour, absorbed in his work.

We only had one bone, but my grandfather had plenty. He carved decorative patterns on them. Sometimes he made them into small sculptures. Scrimshaw, he called it.

'It was a pastime in the whaling ships,' he said. 'Sailors with time on their hands.'

When I was four or five years old, I used to think that he used granny's bones. It was a good logical conclusion for someone so young. I could see the sequence clearly:

He carved bone, but not very much.

Granny died.

He began to carve lots of bone.

So he'd obviously found a new source.

I didn't like to ask, of course. He was not an easy man to approach. He wasn't unfriendly, it was just that he didn't go out of his way to make you feel at ease. He didn't try to explain things. Just said what he had to say.

I liked to visit him. There was something very satisfying about being there in his house. In the heart of the family, somehow. Just him and me and Granny's bones being turned into curious carvings.

And they were curious. On the medicine chest, a serpent lay, bone-white. On top of the TV, a squid wrestled with a tree. A little hunched raven stood on the windowsill by the front door, slowly weathering and turning green.

Some of them were more obviously pretty – a fawn the size of a mouse; a lily flower; a decorative Celtic knot.

Sometimes he would turn and look at me sharply, watching me watching him, wondering if I was interested in the craft. But I wasn't. I just liked the idea of granny's bones turning into something else. Then the scraps and left-overs got thrown in the bin, and that was all right too.

I eventually realised that, however satisfying the idea, the bones most likely just came from the butcher. Some of them were obviously too big to come from granny. I still enjoyed visiting him and seeing him working away with his knives and scrapers. Years passed. The house filled up with carvings.

There's a hiatus then, while I go away and spend time else-where: university, North Africa, several jobs. When I came back, he was still carving. Though his hands were thinner and slower, he was more skilful. I asked him where the fawn was, the sleeping fawn.

'Threw it away. I went back and looked at it one day and I didn't think much of it. I did another one. It's …' He stopped and thought. 'It's on the windowsill at the top of the stairs. Where it catches the sun.'

'You know,' I said, 'I used to think you were carving

Granny's bones.' I laughed, but he didn't. He turned his sharp look on me.

'What made you think that?'

'Just a notion I took. After granny died you did a lot more carving.' I shrugged. 'I was young. It was a silly idea.'

'Well, well, well. That was very perceptive of you.'

'What? Come on, they're not really Granny's bones! She didn't have enough for all this.' I gestured round the room.

'No, that's true. But if they're not from her, they're all for her.'

'Ah.' We seemed to be talking our way into a delicate area. I coughed and asked if I should make a cup of tea. He ignored me.

'She wasn't easy to live with, you know. A strong woman.'

'Oh? Are you sure you don't want a cup of tea?'

He shook his head. 'We had the most terrible arguments.' He smiled. 'She won most of them, I think.' I just waited for him to go on. 'But when she was dead, I missed her – and I even missed the arguments. Strange, eh?'

He was looking at the carving in his fist, not at me.

'After she died, I picked up my tools one day, and all I could think about was that damned smug look on her face when she knew she was in the right. Even though I knew it would do no good, I couldn't help getting angry at her. And that's when a strange thing happened. I put all my anger into the bone. I used the carving to answer her.' He looked up at me then, and smiled again. 'And she couldn't answer back!'

I laughed. He looked like a mischievous boy. I gestured around the room at all the white carvings. 'You must have had a lot of arguments.'

'Yes, we did. And as I remembered all the arguments we had, I started new conversations – and new arguments. These things I've made, they're all the things I never had a chance to say to her. Partly because she never gave me the chance, and partly because there's things that you just can't say in words.'

He bent over his work and after a while I went for a walk round the house, looking at the bone figures in a different way. Some of them were recognisable, now that I knew who they were. Here was Granny's stern and solid hand lying on a windowsill, clenched. That miniature hen scurrying away – she must have just shouted at it. I wondered if Granddad was the hen. The serpent still lay on the medicine chest, and I wondered what that meant. And that was what the house was like: some parts were so clearly my granny that I could almost hear her voice, but most of them were pictures of someone much more complex than I had ever known.

'I'll take that tea now,' he said when I came back into the living room.

I brought through tea and biscuits and put them out on the table, brushing aside the dust and shards of bone.

'Have a look at this,' he said. 'Made it from the top of a thigh bone. A good solid lump.' He handed it up to me.

It was a hooded figure in a robe, beautifully finished. Even the folds in the cloth were burnished. The robe covered the entire body, but the feet poked out from beneath the hem. The toes were precisely detailed, each toenail distinct, even on the little toe.

He leaned forward, holding out his hand. There was a scrap of wire wool in it. 'I used this for the toes,' he whispered. 'I know they didn't have wire wool on the whaling ships, but hell, it's the best way to finish the little details.'

I turned it round to look at the face. It was hidden deep in the cowl, and it was rough, unpolished and distinctly malevolent.

I looked at him.

He looked back at me. 'Well?'

'Well, it's … I don't know. It's not her, is it?'

'Oh aye. That's her all right. Smooth and beautiful on the outside, strong as an axe on the inside.'

I shuddered.

'Her blood runs in your veins, you know. And all the better for it.'

'But she looks dreadful.'

'Aye. But that's the way she was. That's the way people are.'

I looked him over and tried to imagine him like this, dark and fierce inside. He nodded.

'I had a whole lifetime before you came along. I wasn't a grandfather all my days.' Then his eyes settled on my face and I looked back, and we didn't say anything for a long time.

'I'd better be going,' I said.

'You haven't finished your tea.'

It had grown cold. I picked it up and swallowed it at a gulp, then walked to the door. He struggled out of his chair and came with me. Strangely, he shook my hand as I left. He'd never done that before and I'm sure he meant something by it.

Granddad died, as is the way. I was sad, for a while, but he had left me with such a conundrum that it almost felt as if he was still there, looking me in the eye and telling me about Granny and him.

So I went back for the funeral and afterwards, at his house, I took a couple of his sculptures: the fawn asleep and the cowled figure with the savage face. I took his tools too, the homemade scrapers and the knives with wooden handles. 'Made from an old saw,' he told me once. 'Best steel you can get.'

And before I left, I went to see my mum and dad, and I climbed up to Margaret's room at the top of the house. She was working in Glasgow now, but her room was as she'd left it. It didn't take much searching to find the bone, and I took it away with me.

Looking out of my own window, I can see the lights of the city spreading out to left and right as far as I can see, but directly in front, the lights reach an edge, and stop. The sea. One or two small lights move out there – boats, far out and going further.

On the windowsill sit the two carvings I took from Grandad's house: one to remember him and one to remember Granny. Because, no matter whom he made them for, each one is a picture of him too.

And that's where I work on the bone, carving one head out of each end. One for him and one for her. I'm not very good at carving, but they will do. They'll say what they need to say. Two people completely separate, but joined together.

When the carving is done, it's time for the melodrama. A long train journey back home, then into the graveyard at dead of night, with a spade. I find their gravestone and carefully cut out a turf and dig a trench. I drop the bone in and cover it over, stamping the turf back into place. In a day or two, no-one would guess it had been disturbed. The sky is overcast and a small rain is falling. I put out my torch and let the dark come back.

It is as black as the grave. The night has its paws on my eyes, but I am not afraid.

# Carrying the Light

Andrew watched the ants on the windowsill. They moved to and fro on an invisible trail, widely spaced, so that only a half-dozen were visible at a time. They came in at the corner of the window frame, where it had warped away from the wall-beam; they walked across the cedar sill – he bent to sniff it: yes, it was cedar – then down the timber wall and under Chantal's bed.

Ants, he thought. What are they coming in here for? He watched them carefully, but they seemed to leave the room as unburdened as they entered it. They must be carrying something useful. Ants did not frivolously march across bedrooms. He peered closer, but it was difficult to tell. They were very small ants, and not many. But should there be ants in a hotel? Should he mention it to anyone? The manager?

There was a knock on the door and it opened without a pause. There was the manager. On cue. Andrew was interested in coincidences, but no longer surprised by them. They happened too often.

'Hello,' said the manager. Not, 'Hello, sahib.' Kashmir was much more egalitarian than the rest of India.

Andrew raised a hand and let it drop. The manager shut the door behind him. At least, Andrew thought it was the manager. There seemed to be a handful of men running the Parvati Lodge, all of them young and very similar in appearance. Brothers? Cousins? Family, anyway. One of them was called Amin.

'You like the room?'

'It's fine, Amin. Good view.'

Mountainside, heavily wooded, was visible two miles away across the valley. A wedge of blue sky, between two mountains, stretched up past the window frame.

The manager sat down on Chantal's bed.

'My name is Jamil. Amin is my brother.'

'Jamil. Of course.'

'You like Pahalgam?'

'Good place.'

95

The conversation seemed to have finished. Andrew wondered if he should mention the ants.

The manager turned to him.

'You have hashish?'

Andrew didn't know what to say. He looked suspiciously at Jamil, who smiled at him. His eyes were dark and mysterious, impenetrable. Andrew wished Chantal was here. She knew how to deal with hustlers and – well, people. But she was down the hill, in the village, trying to hire a tent. At times like this, Andrew felt far from home. Better be careful.

'No.'

'I get.' Jamil stood and left the room. Andrew leant back against the wall. What now? He didn't want to spend an afternoon stoned with a stranger. God, they barely even had a language in common. The manager's English was adequate, but he didn't seem to use it to do anything but answer questions about the cost of rooms or to ask if they wanted tea.

Two days here and already Andrew wanted to be moving again. What the hell was this travelling for? There must be some reason for it. There had been some reason at the beginning – there must have been. It had taken him years to nerve himself up to it, and then he'd given up a good job. It wasn't easy to do – he'd never even left Britain before.

Whatever the reason was, he'd been travelling for eight weeks: 3,000 miles overland to get somewhere or to find something. He wished he could find it. Perhaps tomorrow he could convince Chantal to move on. Or maybe she'd prefer to stay here and he would go on alone. He could manage that better now. India was so terrifyingly vast at first. It had been good to find a travelling companion. Chantal had spotted him at the bus station in Amritsar, trying to buy a ticket to Pathankot. He kept getting edged out of the queue, and no-one would listen to him.

'*Trop de politesse*,' she said. 'You are too nice. Do it like this.'

She shouted at the ticket clerk until they got the right ticket, then they went together to a chai-shop. 'Hey! Chai here!' She shouted as she and Andrew pushed their way to a table. A boy

brought them two glasses of tea. She sipped at it and looked at
Andrew. 'Nobody goes to Pathankot,' she said. 'Only to pass
through. You go then to Kashmir?'

'Yes.'

'I have hassle in India.' She pulled a face. 'Woman alone,
always hassle hassle hassle. *Merde*. It is too much trouble. You
go to Kashmir, I go also. *Nous allons ensemble, hein?* We go
together. Okay?'

After just a few days in India, Andrew felt that his decisions
and plans had begun to be irrelevant. Nothing he planned ever
worked out as it should. India was a pinball machine and he
was the steel ball. He'd just taken to accepting whatever came
to him. Now Chantal had come to him with her long hennaed
hair and her French accent and her no-nonsense proposal.

'Okay.'

And since then, they'd come this far together. To Pahalgam,
far in the north of Kashmir. A conjunction of paths, that was
all. Fellow travellers. She had her own reasons for being here,
but they'd never discussed the matter.

Andrew kept his reasons to himself too, because he simply
couldn't tell her.

He'd come all the way to Kashmir, to the valley of
Pahalgam, intending to visit the holy cave of Siva, far away
in the mountains. Then he'd discovered that the passes would
be snowbound until July or August. Three or four months.
Chantal knew so much more than he did about travelling,
about India, everything. He'd never be able to admit the truth
to her.

Not that it made any difference. It was time to go. He could
feel it, the impatience humming inside him, the urge to go
somewhere, to do something.

The door opened and the manager entered, carrying a water-
pipe. Andrew automatically slipped his shoes off and tucked
his feet up on the bed. The dynamics of the room changed.
Now there was a bed on which people could sit, instead of a
bed on which Andrew was sitting.

Jamil sat on the bed beside him, tucking his feet under the
loose folds of his trousers. He struck a match and drew on the

pipestem, the water bubbling in the flask. The thick sweet smell seemed too rich. Andrew had no stomach for it. He decided to refuse it. Jamil passed the pipe to him. He took it and sucked on the stem. Andrew could hear a small argument in a room downstairs. Outside, hens clucked. He breathed out slowly.

'Shiva!'

Jamil smiled as he took the pipe.

'Shambu!'

When the pipe was out, Jamil put it on the floor by the bed and tugged at the corner of the rug to straighten it. He turned to Andrew.

'Good room,' he said.

Andrew could feel the textures of the wood around him just by looking. He could feel the pile of the carpet, and the breeze on his face from the open window. A buffalo bellowed on the hillside nearby.

'Good room,' he agreed. But should he mention the ants? He gestured to the windowsill.

Jamil stood and leant over the windowsill. 'Ah.' He put out a finger to touch an ant. It stopped and wiggled its antennae, then it turned, hunting for something. It found the scent trail and continued on its way. Another tiny ant came along the track. It reached the finger and waggled its antennae, then it moved away to find the trail.

People were laughing on the grass in front of the hotel, Kashmiri accents and German and English. A bird called, a brazen cry like a cock pheasant.

On the opposite side of the valley, a train of ponies made their way up the track towards the higher meadows and the snowline. They seemed about to bump into Jamil's finger, where he held it upright on the sill. Andrew moved his head to get a clear view. A Kashmiri was leading the first horse, on which sat a fat man, probably a tourist. The other horses carried panniers, luggage and provisions. They turned a bend in the track, so that the horses seemed to bunch up, one after the other until there was one blocky beast of many parts with the tourist sitting on its front part.

A kite swung slowly across the valley, its wings spread wide.

It was a thousand feet high, but it was just about level with the hotel window. Andrew felt himself drawn into the space outside. Without seeing it, he could still see the valley opening out southwards, growing wider and lower, until it met the huge valley up which the bus had brought them two days before. The willow groves that flanked the road leaned with the warm wind and shook in the turbulence of the bus passing close by. Branches whipped a signboard beside a wooden warehouse.

'Shankar Cricket Bats' it said, and underneath, 'From 1937 – Finest of Kashmir Willow.' There had been signs like that beside the road every few miles since they'd come into the merely huge valley up which the bus had turned from the truly enormous Vale of Kashmir. Down in the Vale of Kashmir lay the city of Srinagar, its canals with barges and house boats, and lake Dal, shallow and reedy, with floating neighbourhoods of house boats, some only family homes, others large enough to be hotels. At evening, a flat-bottomed boat floated out to the Golden Palace Hotel, laden with Andrew and Chantal and bags of provisions.

They'd been out there on the lake with darkness coming down and boat lights gleaming around about. The city of Srinagar faded into the night as they poled away from it. Stars were coming out, big and bright, so that the horizon was lost, and there was just a firmament of lights, with their boat floating through it, lit by a hissing naphtha lamp on an upright pole.

One of the lights was moving closer to them, the lamp shining down, the pole invisible in the darkness. A face gleamed in the lamplight, looking towards them, but the boatman was hidden, only the end of his pole glowing in the light as he brought it forward, sliding back into the night as he pushed.

'Hey, sahib!'

Chantal muttered to Andrew. 'Watch out. Hustler. Kashmiris only say "Sahib" when they're selling something.'

The face in the other boat turned towards the invisible boatman and the light slowed, then came closer, accompanied by the gurgle of the water at the bow.

They pulled alongside. Most of the boat was filled with bales of cloth, but the man sitting among them was selling hashish.

He held it out on his palm and Andrew looked at it. It was soft and black and sticky.

'*Non. Pas maintenant.* We will get some at another time,' said Chantal.

The dealer, knowing his trade, looked at Andrew. Andrew lifted the hashish and sniffed it, purely for the sake of form. He was enchanted by this encounter in the starry night, only two boats and their cargoes in the entire perceptible universe, while the lights shone above, around and below, reflecting in the black water.

'How much? How many rupees?'

And before that there was the long ride up from Pathankot.

Pathankot. A grim town. They rented a grimy expensive room in the Bus Station And Railway Transport Hotel. Both he and Chantal were afflicted by a stomach bug.

The heat was thick in the hotel room, clogging the air, but at least the shower was working. They took turns at the shower, cooling down briefly each time, then swamped by the heat once again, until the water was turned off at nine o' clock. Then it was just the heat and the mosquitoes. And many trips to the toilet, using the fading torch because the electricity was off too.

Then the next morning, lost in the pandemonium of the bus station: one tiny ticket office with three windows and enormous queues at each. The overworked ticket clerk only waved vaguely when they asked where the bus was. Andrew and Chantal, sweating and harried among the crowds, a bewildering mass of shouting, screaming people: family groups, traders with bundles of goods, farmers from the hills with two hens hanging upside down from one hand, bicycle rickshaws pushing through, shouting for trade – and the buses, buses, buses, with only the smudged numbers on their tickets to guide them.

Then sudden cramps. One of them has to go to the toilet, urgently. Going together, because they'd never find each other again. Pushing through the crowds to the public toilets and finding them choked and overflowing with shit and piss. Then the toilet attendant, sitting outside on the ground playing cards with his cronies, stands up, holds out his hand and asks for baksheesh.

Chantal going crazy, shouting and screaming at him in French then, when she remembers, in English. 'How is it possible? You idiot, you sheet-head! How is it possible you can ask me for baksheesh?'

The man shrugged his shoulders then turned to smile and shrug at his friends. They shook their heads in sympathy.

Chantal grabbed him by the shoulder and dragged him into the toilet, shouting and pointing with her free hand at the overflowing sewage and the spreading brown and yellow puddles.

'Thees! You see thees! For thees you ask baksheesh? Baksheesh in your focking face!' And then she was back into French and Andrew had to lay hold of her and pull her out, because if he had to stay another minute in that baking sewage pit he'd have fainted, and he could hear as clear as day the splat he'd make on the floor.

On the bus at last, they slumped and practised dynamic tension on the belly and sphincter muscles while the bus ground its way into the hills beyond Pathankot. Finally they stopped at a battered tin building where dirty glass beakers sat on tables in the full sun. Flies sucked the table for spilt sugar. A man wiped one glass with his dirty turban-end, then gave up, tucked the cloth away and began to pour tea and collect money.

Andrew and Chantal slipped away behind some bushes to relieve themselves. They were not the first to use the spot, but it was a good deal cleaner than the Pathankot toilets.

After that, the bus climbing hour after hour, the hillsides growing steeper, the long hairpin bends tighter, the moistness of the foothills drying out. All the windows in the bus are open, but the heat in the bus is still intense, though bearable now that it is less humid. Then at last, the bus skirts a mountain and plunges into a tunnel, long and dark. Andrew expecting more of the same at the other end, but numbed into patience, just waiting it out until they get where they're going.

The light at the end of the tunnel growing brighter, growing, until blip! Out into the light. For an instant there is just brightness, then details spring out: broken stone at the roadside for road repairs, and an elephant having its panniers filled with rock, its handler standing in front of it.

They both turn to watch the elephant, and while they are looking the bus rounds a slope, so that when they look back, they are flying into Kashmir, flying out into green, the green valley of Kashmir wide as sight, edged with the knees of mountains so high you have to look up. And God, the cool wind! There was such a caress in the wind. The brown earth and dust of the plains and foothills is gone. Grass grows here, and bushes and trees.

Even days later, Andrew can feel the balm of that moment. There was suddenly a point to being there, there were suddenly possibilities in the world other than death by dysentery or melting into a spot of grease.

In the bus, Chantal and he grinned at each other. They were friends for a moment, not just travelling companions.

He sighed, remembering the feeling.

'Small earth animals,' Jamil said softly, turning from the ants on the windowsill. His eyes were dark and deep, mysterious, but without shadows.

Andrew nodded. 'Small earth animals,' he agreed.

The ants moved along their trail, one way and another. Finding something useful and bringing it back.

# Backwaters

'Hello? Hello, are you there?'
    It's a good question, and I try to answer.

The doctor is pompous and expansive, pleased with himself and his own cleverness. 'Look at that hillside,' he says. 'Isn't that a magnificent sight? Landseer would have loved to paint that. Don't you think so?'

I am the ghillie. I'm supposed to know where the fish lie, where to take the boat so that he'll stand a chance of catching a sea-trout. I do know these things – and I also know how to find excuses for his poor angling. That's my job too. 'The clouds are too low today,' I might say, or, 'The clouds are too high.' But his self-satisfied complacency annoys me. I don't always let him have his own way.

'Landseer,' I say, thoughtfully. 'Perhaps. But look at that pine tree on the cliff there, shaped by the wind. I can just see Hiroshige drawing that.'

'Hiroshige,' he says, and frowns, as if thinking about it. 'In oils, d'you think?'

'Sumi-e,' I say. 'Japanese ink,' then say no more, sick of the game. It makes me feel diminished, reacting to his petty arrogance. I change the subject. 'Maybe we should try Witches Point?' I suggest. 'With the wind from the east there's a fair chance of finding a fish there.'

The sun shone down for most of that summer. The doctor caught few fish – but neither did anyone else on the loch. Most of the fishermen resigned themselves to the good weather and spent more time over lunch than they did on the water. I slipped into a trance in the middle of June, and even the doctor could not rouse me from my imperturbable bliss.

I sit in the boat and pull on the oars. Water drips from the blades, rippling the silvery mirror of the loch. I don't expect to go anywhere, it is just the action which I have to perform. Like chanting a mantra, like singing a song, like dancing. It doesn't have a purpose. It is its own purpose. These, and other things, I think about, hanging there between two infinities: the blue sky above and the blue sky below. Each slow sweep of the oars is taking me deeper and deeper below the surface, while it moves the boat hardly at all. The days are so bright that the fish are hiding their silver away, panting for breath in the cool dark depths. With the weather like this, we will never catch anything – but the doctor still has his rod out.

The loch is not a perfect mirror. Close to the boat, where shadow falls on the water, it is possible to see through the surface. Sometimes I see rocks and weeds, sometimes it appears that I am looking into endless depths. If I turn the boat – slowly, so that the doctor doesn't notice – I can see my own silhouette, and with the sun behind me, it appears that I have a dark twin in the water, who has a nimbus of sunlight around him. I am so far gone that I feel no self-consciousness in imagining that I am a demi-god in a mythical boat: the Maori progenitor sailing the sea of stars or Gilgamesh crossing to the land beyond the waters. Even dark Charon, ferrying souls. In the brightness of that summer, it is easy to think of such things, and in the evening, when I lie in the bothy waiting for sleep, the day's light still fills me and I float into the netherworlds without any sense of transition.

The doctor is a phenomenon. When I manage not to be irritated by him, he's amusing. His mind is small and bounded by an impenetrable ignorance. But because of this, he doesn't even notice when he's out of his depth. I think of Wily Coyote walking out into thin air – only, unlike Coyote, the doctor never does the double-take, never notices what he's doing – and so he never falls. One day he asks, 'What do you think you are doing with your life?' He has decided I need a talking-to.

'Living it.' It sounds glib, but I can't think what else to say.

'Yes, yes.' He sounds disgusted. 'But what are you doing with your opportunities? Your talents. You're a bright lad. Why not go back to college? You could be whatever you want. A teacher. A doctor.'

'Why do you think I'm here?' I gesture around, including the hills, the islands and the small clouds that are drifting in from the east and burning away into nothing; including the loch that seems to hold all of these in its magic mirror, supporting us in this boat on the invisible water. Invisible? Yes, it is. Look at it all you will, you will not see water, but only the image of the sky and the hills. Apart from the doctor, there is nothing here that I would wish to change. And even the doctor, after a while, has become less of an irritant. There are midges here, too, and I can put up with them.

'*Force majeure*,' he says, dismissively.

I smile and say no more. He can't understand that this job isn't meant to lead to anything else. This moment is where I have wanted to be all of my life. When time has passed, as it surely will, this is still where I am. Time does not apply to this summer.


'We're going to try to move you. Hello, are you there?'

I am there, and I try to tell them so.


I woke in the night and I was out of the bunk and heading up the companionway before I was properly awake. I could sense two other figures in the darkness, both struggling out of their bedclothes. I threw open the door and stuck my head out.

'Thump!' That was the sound that had wakened me. The boat rolled and threw me sideways. My head smacked against mahogany, crushing my ear.

'Oh shit!'

Against the moonlit sky, I could see our mast clearly, a black stripe swinging wildly across gleaming clouds. I clambered out onto the tilting deck, Gavin pushing his way out behind me, Dave muttering behind him, struggling into his survival suit.

'Right,' said Gavin. His eyes were bleary with sleep. 'Quick assessment, Alex. What's the situation?'

I almost laughed, but there was another thump and the boat began to sway in the other direction. I grabbed a hand-hold. 'The tide's dropped,' I said, 'and our keel's hitting the rocks.'

Gavin turned to Dave. 'Dave?'

'What?'

'What's our situation, Dave?'

'Haven't a fucking clue. Are we on the rocks?'

'Phthoomp!' The boat juddered and swayed.

'It appears so. Thank god there's no wind.'

'Just this bloody swell.'

Four foot waves were rolling in from the Atlantic, slow and gentle. But each one, as it passed, gently lifted six tons of yacht then dropped it on the rocks again.

'Right.' Gavin's eyes were jittering about, but his voice was controlled, like a schoolmaster containing his anger. 'Suggestions?'

'Wait till she's on the top of a wave and motor out, full throttle.'

'We're not going to drift in, are we?' Dave peered anxiously towards the black-on-black rocky shore, only thirty yards away.

Gavin glanced once, then back again. 'Not while we're on two anchors.'

'We'll have to lift them,' I said, 'if we're going to motor out.'

Gavin looked at me and shook his head. 'I can't risk motoring over the rocks. Damage the keel.'

'Thump!' There was a dreadful groaning sound as the keel grated on the rocks below.

'More than that?'

Gavin's eyes flickered around, looking for some way out. His jaw was trembling.

'And it's going to get worse,' I said. 'We're not at low tide yet.'

Gavin bit his lip. His brow wrinkled ferociously, then cleared. 'Dave! Down below. Get the tide-tables. We'd better know the worst. All right, then, Alex. Lift the stern anchor now!'

The anchor was usually a two-man job. As the boat shuddered and swayed, and the mast swung across the heavens, I took hold of the anchor chain and hauled, then hauled again, not trying to stow the chain, just letting it fall to the deck. The tiller walloped against the hull as the wave caught it, then I had to drop the chain as the tiller arm scythed across.

I grabbed again and pulled, and pulled. Nothing happened. 'Dave! Dave! Give me a hand!'

Dave threw the tide-tables to Gavin in the cabin and came over. We both hauled, but the chain would come in no further. As the boat lifted on the next wave, the rusty chain pulled back through my hands.

'It's stuck! Gavin, the anchor's fouled!'

The motor was running now, coughing loudly each time a wave lifted the exhaust into the air. Gavin came across and we all pulled. Nothing happened. I looked at Gavin for guidance. His eyes were jumping about crazily. His mouth opened but nothing came out. The keel thumped, the boat groaned. 'Ditch the anchor!' he said. 'Alex, go aft and unfasten the chain shackle. But don't let the chain go yet!'

I dashed below deck and found the shackle down in the bilges, where the anchor chain was fastened. I wrenched at the pin until it turned and came loose. 'Chain's free,' I called as I scrambled up on to the steep deck.

From the wheelhouse Gavin called: 'Let go!'

Dave kicked at the chain and it roared through its mounting and disappeared into the depths.

'The forward anchor now, boys! Haul on it when I hit the throttle!'

Dave and I ran forward and took hold of the chain. We waited until the boat lifted on a wave and then we pulled, while Gavin revved the motor. There was a scraping sound, and he cut the throttle. 'She won't do it!' There was distress in his voice.

'Give her welly,' I shouted back. 'You can't do any worse than the waves!'

His face looked agonized. The boat thumped and swayed again. 'One more time then. Ready?'

'Aye.'

'Yes.'

'Then go!'

The engine roared and the boat grated its way forward a foot or two, slowed, then stopped. Dave and I hauled on the chain and Gavin gave the motor full throttle. Nothing more happened, except that the wave in its own good time dropped us once more onto the rock.

There was nothing left to do but wait for the tide to turn. We unshipped the spare jib and used it to try to hold us steady, pushing it down through the water until it touched bottom. We had to do it in shifts, because fifteen minutes was enough to exhaust any one of us. After half an hour or so, Dave managed to sneak below to fetch his cigarettes, but his hands were shaking so much he couldn't light up. I leaned against him so that we could stay steady on the rocking deck and held the lighter while he tried to get the cigarette into the flame.

We had eighty minutes until the tide turned, and then another hundred or so until it would rise high enough for us to get off. Every few seconds, the boat thumped and groaned and rolled. Every few seconds Gavin's face grew tight and his voice would falter as the rocks below gouged at the keel of his boat.

Daylight came. The sky was azure and clear; the waves rolled in, beautiful and smooth. We could see the shore now, and the Isle of Eigg, with its magnificent mountain rising almost straight out of the sea. We were saying nothing now, just grimly taking turns on the wooden jib, trying to keep the boat stable.

At 4.30am, Gavin tried the motor again and with Dave and me pulling on the anchor chain, we came free. I bowed my head and just stood there as we motored out to a safe distance. I don't know about Gavin and Dave, but I was weeping with relief. When I had recovered, I looked around. Dave's face was grey with exhaustion. Gavin was shaking his head and trying to smile.

'Thanks, lads,' he said. 'That ... that was a bad one. Well done.'

Dave nodded and opened his mouth, but nothing came out.

'Dave, you get off to your bunk. Alex, we'd better see to your hands before anything else.'

I looked at my hands. They were raw and blistered – from the chain running through them, then several hours trying to hold the boat up with a wooden pole. 'I didn't notice...'

'Your ear's pretty bad too, but we'll just have to wait for that to go down.'

I remembered banging it, a long, long time ago. I shrugged.

Gavin and I sat by the stern and talked, while he bandaged my hands. My ear was throbbing like a complete bastard, I told Gavin, now that it had been drawn to my attention.

I thought we might lose her, he told me, while he tied bandages, with his head bowed over my hands. He sniffed a couple of times and turned to look at the sun coming up out of the Minch.

I put a bandaged hand on his shoulder. 'You know the worst bit?' I asked.

'No. What was that?'

'I don't ever, ever want to be in that kind of situation again. Because when you're under pressure, you sound just like my old schoolmaster. And it's fucking dreadful!'

'You did well,' he said, when we'd stopped laughing. 'Now, down below, you. I'll keep watch.'

'Nah, nah. I'm wide awake now. Anyway, there's work to be done. The tiller arm.' I pointed. Sometime in the night, with the tiller banging about, the wooden shaft had snapped.

'Oh hell! We haven't got a spare – and I don't think we've got the tools to fix it.'

'Oh no?' I reached into my pocket and pulled out my Swiss army knife.

'Never!' he said.

'Oh yes,' I said. 'Off to your bed, skipper, and I'll have a working tiller ready for you when you wake.'

They slept till noon, while I sat on the after hatch and whittled away at the tiller shaft with a blunt penknife. I sang quietly to myself and watched nothing at all happening: waves passing, seabirds flying, the sun moving up the sky. Clouds came up and a rain began to fall.

'O western wind when wilt though blow, that the small rain down may rain,' I sang.

I could feel my hands stinging under their bandages and my ear was hot and throbbing. My legs were stiff from sitting too long on the wooden deck – but the small rain was hissing on the long grey waves, and I wanted nothing that I didn't have. I was here, right here, and that was all right. Part of me thought that was an awfully simple-minded way to look at the world, but the rest of me was happy, so I left it unexamined.

'Hello?'

I can hear a voice speaking to me.

'Hello? Are you there?'

There is the most dreadful pain. It is a wall, it is a mountain. I cannot contain it. I turn away from these mountains of pain. I know what it means, and there is no need to investigate further. There are bits of me in places where they shouldn't be. There are addresses in my mind, in my picture of myself, that don't mean anything any more.

'Hello, are you there?'

I know they're speaking to me and I know they can't hear my thoughts, but I am thinking at them as hard as I can – Yes, I'm there.

'We're going to try to move you,' the voice says.

Sunlight fills the valley. Sunlight grazes the surface of the loch, and it bounces. What makes it bounce? Water. What is water? I don't know, but whatever it is, this is my stuff: if I was in charge of the world, if I was God, this is what I would do with light. A deep thrill goes through me. I feel tears spring to my eyes. I want to call out in a loud voice, I want to let my voice say what I feel, in a long, long cry that will fill this space –

'Mum,' I say. 'Mum?'

'Yes?'

'I feel...'

'Cold, hmm?' She tucks my scarf inside my jacket and

buttons it up. 'Won't be long now and we can go home.'

The sun is sliding below the horizon, no more warm, now, than a distant fire. Wind comes off the sea and goes through me. I can feel every part of me shiver with the salt and the spray and the thinness of the world. I can see through it, I could reach through it. But even in this threadbare world, the water is real. It is all the way through the world, all through it and into me.

'I'm not cold,' I say, trying to explain.

She smiles and rubs the back of her hand against my cheek, fondly. But what she is fond of is not me. Not just now.

She takes my hand and I give in and let myself be what she is fond of. But as we walk up the hill to the house and teatime, I keep looking back at whatever it was that I saw, until, some time between tea and bed, I grow tired and I forget.

Hello, are you there?

Yes, I am there.

And it is true. I am there. Water is everywhere that life is, and where water is, that is where I am.

# The End of the Octopus

# The End of the Octopus

'We need more milk,' Kay says firmly, and I wince.
It is true that we are low on milk – but I'm flinching from the tone she uses, that firm, confident tone that she used to use for important things: confronting someone about an important issue or facing down someone who thought their uniform gave them the right to bully her or her friends. When the point was that we'd need three pints of milk on Saturday, with the family coming to tea, it was heartbreakingly sad to hear.

I feel a sudden pang of affection for her, remembering who she was, and who she presumably still is, inside. Tears spring to my eyes and I put my arms around her. She tolerates the embrace for half a second, then frowns at me. 'What do you want?' she asks sharply and turns away to pick up the TV remote and fiddle with it.

The channels change a couple of times then return to the nature programme. The fuzzy blueness of the sea is full of octopi, hundreds of them chasing through the water, swooping with their legs bunching and trailing behind them, holding each other with their many arms, mating in their cool and alien underwater passion.

'The octopus is not the only sea animal to respond in this way,' says the calm and reassuring voice of the commentator. The picture changes to show determined turtles swimming in their Paleolithic way towards some far-off beach.

'I think I'll make some tea,' she says firmly.

'I shan't argue with that,' I say, before I can stop myself.

She frowns. 'Why would you? I presume that's your graceful way of saying that you'd like a cup, too.'

I nod and grunt in agreement. 'Will you look at that,' I say, gesturing at the TV. There is nothing of any interest showing. She turns to look.

'What, the sea?'

'No, it was…' I say, then shrug. 'Never mind, it's gone now.'

She is suspicious, I can see she is, but she lets it go.

'Tea,' she says, and goes through to the kitchen. The door is half-open, and through the gap I can see her at the sink, then by the kettle. There is no hint that there is anything on her mind but making the tea. Why should there be? Yet I am sad.

The outside door bangs open and Steve comes in. Kay turns from the sink and peers, as if she is wondering who it might be, though it could only be Steve.

'Hi, Mum.'

'Where have you been to this hour?'

Steve goes to the bread bin and rakes through it. 'Out. It's not late.'

'I know.' Her voice has softened. 'I just like to know what you're doing.'

'Oh, this and that.' He puts jam on a slice of bread and folds it over into a makeshift sandwich. 'Went to see Ian and Greg. Haven't seen them in months.'

She is standing in front of him now, straightening his shirt collar. I almost expect her to wipe the blob of jam from his face, but that would be absurd, with him being a head taller than she is.

'Jam,' she says, pointing to the corner of his mouth. His tongue licks out to clean it up. 'We're just having a cup of tea,' she says firmly.

He nods slowly, waiting to see what it has to do with him. When she says no more, he forces the last of his sandwich into his mouth. 'Just going up to my room,' he mumbles around the bread.

'Steven! That's no way to eat.'

Then he is gone and the kettle is boiling.

After the dance at the Student Union, we went back to the flat and sat around in the kitchen. It was quite nice, as student flats went – a bit grubby and untidy, with the usual selection of humorous or arty posters on the walls. It suited us. Most of us were probably a bit grubby too, and scruffily dressed in the usual student mix of jeans and tat from the charity shops.

Except for Deirdre. Her clothes may have come from a

charity shop, but she wore them with style. Everyone else in the kitchen was sitting, but she was standing, and her long black skirt emphasized her height. The glossy black wings of her hair swung as her head moved, alternately hiding and revealing the smooth skin of her neck and the thin black choker with a single gem set in it – probably not a diamond, but with Deirdre, who knew?

There was something of the Pre-Raphaelite look about her and that fine face hid a keen mind – but did not hide it too deeply. She was usually the most intelligent person in the room, and didn't care if you knew it.

All in all, she was enough to make a young man sigh. I certainly did, but nothing more. She was too sophisticated, different from the rest of us, and unattainable.

Kay, on the other hand, the only other unattached woman in the room, was too much like one of us. She was small and pretty, with curling red hair. She was sweet and friendly, but somehow unexceptional – like the sister of a best friend. She was always somewhere around, but usually unnoticed.

Two men with long hair were sitting at the kitchen table, listening to a late-night programme on Radio 1. One of them was rolling a joint. On the sofa, a couple sat. She held his arm with both hands, watching his face and glancing round at the rest of us from time to time. A woman was trying to make coffee for those as wanted, holding the switch down on the kettle because it popped back up if you let go. I was slumped in an easy chair and Kay was in the window seat, looking out through her reflection at the streetlights and the wet roofs spread out down the hill towards the river.

The room was, for the moment, silent, except for the rising hum of the kettle and the music from the radio.

'All interaction between men and women is based on sex,' said Deirdre, and everyone looked at her. 'Good manners, politeness – they're fuelled by the desire to reproduce. If he had no desire to procreate, no man would ever give up his seat to a woman or pay for her lunch. Courtesy is a sham.'

I winced at that, since I had carefully held the door open for her when we came into the flat. The man on the couch nodded, as if agreeing – or perhaps just so that he wouldn't have to say anything. Kay was frowning thoughtfully. Deirdre looked around at us, waiting for a response. Finally her gaze settled on me and she raised one eyebrow sardonically.

'There's something to be said for that,' I said.

Kay glanced at me then looked up at Deirdre, whose mouth was opening, just about to continue. 'That's not so,' Kay said. Her eyes were bright and her face determined.

Deirdre looked a little taken aback, as if she wasn't used to being challenged. 'I rather think that it is,' she replied. 'Sadly, there is little more to our social structure than various more or less subtle expressions of the mating instinct.'

'There are many factors involved.' Kay spoke, her words very precise, as if she didn't want to say it, but had to do so in the interests of truth. 'Some of them are less obvious than sex, some of them are so obvious that they are simply overlooked. Survival, benevolence, enlightened self-interest, transcendence.'

To my surprise, Deirdre actually seemed to waver. 'I think you'll find that most people in the field...' she began.

'I think Deirdre is right,' I said, and shrugged. 'Sex and the desire for it can explain loads of human behaviour.'

Kay turned to look directly at me. Her eyes were still bright, her cheeks a little flushed. She spoke firmly, as if telling me something that really I ought to know, if I just stopped to think for a moment. 'Of course. But it's not the best explanation, just an easy one to work with, for sociologists with little imagination and a thesis to write.'

I started my next sentence without even knowing where I was going, just so that she'd keep looking at me. 'But what about...' I said, and just kept talking. Another conversation began over at the table. Deirdre had fallen silent and she drifted away as Kay and I argued.

Afterwards, when we knew each other better, I told her that I actually agreed with her. I wasn't arguing just for the sake of it though. I wanted to see that look on her face again and hear that tone in her voice: determined and firm. Fearless. I loved that, the way she drew a line and was ready to defend it.

You can argue about theories forever. It was a more difficult and courageous thing to plant your flag and take a stand, and I told her so.

'It's time Steve was away,' Kay said as she came through with two mugs of tea. 'This place is getting too small for him.'

'Do you think so?'

She frowned at me as if I was being dense. 'Yes. I was just talking to him in the kitchen.'

It just sounded to me like a boy fending off his mother's nosy questions. 'Soon, maybe' I said. 'But not yet.'

She handed me my tea and sat down in her chair. 'Julie was at college by his age.'

'But if he doesn't want...'

'He does want,' she said firmly. 'He's been going round visiting his friends.'

'Yes, but...'

'He's saying goodbye.'

And I can't argue. I used to love that tone of voice, the surety in it. But now that it has become devalued, it is painful to hear it once more – and know that she is right. Steve *is* ready to go, and then the house will be empty except for us.

She turns to watch the TV. The commentator is speaking. 'This female octopus has found herself a niche in the rocks where she hangs, barely moving, arms folded over to cage her mass of eggs. She will not leave her eggs now for any reason and she has stopped eating.'

Kay sips her tea and watches the floating octopus cuddling its eggs.

Now the scene changes and there are sharks, many of them, swirling slowly and menacingly. I don't watch them. I watch Kay, absorbing the fact that she's right, that she sometimes sees things clearly that are a mystery to me.

She turns from the TV and sees me watching her.

'Your tea will get cold,' she says firmly, and I know she is right. My heart sinks.

Julie was unwell. She was lying in her cot, naked, to keep her cool. She whimpered now and then, but seemed too miserable and exhausted to do more. We'd washed her down with a wet flannel, and that had helped for a bit, but now she was hot again, and crying. Kalpol had helped too, but she'd already had as much as we were prepared to give her.

'She needs a doctor,' said Kay. 'Phone the surgery will you. I'll give her another wash down.'

'It's nine o'clock,' I said. 'There won't be anyone there.'

'They'll have an emergency number.'

'All right.'

I phoned the surgery and listened to the message. 'The surgery is closed until 8.30 am. If you have an emergency, please call ...'

I wrote the number down then rang the doctor and told him the situation.

'I'm out on a call at the moment,' he said. 'Bring her round to the surgery. I'll be back there in half an hour.'

'All right.'

I went to the front door and called up the stairs to Kay. 'I'm just going to bring the car round.'

'What for?' Her voice was sharp.

'So we can take Julie to ...'

'Julie's not going anywhere. Tell the doctor to come here.'

'But Kay, I've just spoken to him and arranged ...'

'Well, call him back and tell him!'

'I can't do that!'

She came down the stairs, almost at a run. 'You watch Julie. I'll call.'

From Julie's bedside I listened in awe as she very calmly and firmly explained to the doctor that she had a sick child, that the child was not going to be moved anywhere and that he, the doctor, was going to come to the house to attend her. After a brief pause, she told him this again, then very obviously interrupted his reply to say, 'Now. Please.' Then she put the phone down.

I stepped back, involuntarily, as she came back into the room. I didn't want to be between her and the baby. We didn't speak at all until the doctor arrived, when I hurried down to open the door for him. He was wearing a grim look compounded of thwarted authority and ill-temper.

'She's upstairs,' I said, and pointed the way, letting him go first.

He did a thorough job of inspecting Julie, while Kay watched his every move. He took some medicine from his black bag and scribbled out a prescription.

'Give her this tonight and get the prescription in the morning. Keep her cool and get her to drink as much as you can.'

'Thank you,' said Kay, firmly.

Downstairs I opened the door. The doctor stopped at the doorway and turned to Kay.

'We do have other patients, you know. It's our job to look after them, too.'

'Of course,' she said, still unbending, completely sure of herself. 'And our concern is with *our* child. That's *our* job.'

He stood still, just for a moment, and looked at her. Then he glanced at me and I could see that despite his bad temper, there was also respect in his face, not having come across such unbending intent too often. I felt sorry for him, but I could feel a small smile on my lips and the surge of some strong emotion in my chest. He slammed the door as he left.

Kay turned to speak to me, then frowned. 'What are you grinning about?'

'Not sure,' I said. 'I think I'm proud of you.'

'I see,' she said, still in her no-nonsense tone. Then she softened. 'Make me a cup of tea, will you? I'm knackered.'

'Back on the reef,' said the commentator, 'The eggs have hatched. The tiny octopi are already searching the nooks and crannies for food. Many of them will, themselves, become food for the other inhabitants of the reef, but there are so many of them that some will survive and grow to maturity.'

The camera focuses on a section of coral where the minuscule hatchlings are flitting about and waving their many legs. Then the camera pulls back to show the mother octopus. Her arms drift in the currents. She is so pale that the rocks can be seen through her.

'Meanwhile, the mother has faded away. Nothing remains but the husk of her body. Only the shape tells us that this was once a living octopus. Yet she has fulfilled her purpose. Her children will grow and populate the reef. Another generation will continue the cycle of life.' Uplifting music plays as the credits roll over a picture of the reef and the tattered wisp of octopus. The camera moves back and back until reef and octopus fade into the ocean blue.

Kay points the remote and clicks a button. The picture disappears.

'That's it over,' she says firmly.

'I think you're right,' I say.

# The Barb

'There was another ghillie on the loch – I forget his name – he told me about the bird.'

She nodded and watched him speak. His lips moved and touched each other, together and apart, as he formed the words. His sun-browned hands were wrapped around his mug. His eyes were fastened on her and his pupils were large and shiny and black.

'He was a bit older than me,' he said. 'He'd worked on the loch for a dozen seasons and he knew where the fish lay, where the channels were among the islands, where to shelter from the weather. But he didn't usually talk a lot.'

She thought about what he was saying. She was imagining the other ghillie. She saw him as an older, wiry man with reddish hair, sipping whisky in the bar and quietly watching the other people.

'I remember he came in to work one time with his hand bandaged. I asked him what happened, and he said he'd been tying flies and got a fish-hook in his thumb.'

'Ouch!' she said.

'And it was in too deep to work it back out.'

'So, did the doctor have to cut it out?'

'It was Saturday night and the doctor lived a dozen miles away. Do you know what he did?'

'He didn't cut it out himself?'

'No. He had a vice that sat on his table, for fly-tying. It was quite heavy. He tied the hook to the vice with a length of gut, then he dropped the vice. The falling weight ripped the hook out.'

'Oh, God!'

'Oh God, indeed. But it worked.'

She shuddered and reflexively curled her fingers around her own thumb, to protect it.

'Anyway, he told me there was a bird living on the North Shore that would fly out to the boat while you were fishing. Not every time, just now and then.'

'Did you ever see it?'

He looked at her and smiled. 'Yes.' There was pleasure in his smile, and wonder, and surprise too, as if he were seeing it all over again. 'Weeks after he'd told me about it. I'd almost forgotten. Then, one day, I had the boat out by the North Shore. It was a beautiful bright day – too bright for fishing, really. There was just a breath of wind, rippling the water.'

He was still for a few seconds, his eyes far away, remembering.

'Tell me about it,' she said.

I could hear the gurgle of the oars, very quiet, as they slid through the water, then the faint sound of drips from the blade and then the pleasant 'cloop' as I dropped the oar into the water once more. Listening really carefully, there were other sounds – a hiss from the breeze blowing past my ear and a little groan as the polished wood of the oar moved in the rowlocks.

It was my job to find the places on the loch where a fish might be hiding, so that my paying guest could catch it. He sat in the bow, with a beaked cap to shade his eyes. His long rod was extended and the fly was dancing slowly across the rippled water. I pulled on the oars slowly and regularly, keeping the boat broadside to the breeze.

Then I saw a small dark shape flying out from the trees that grew right down to the water's edge. I just had the chance to say 'Look!' The bird swooped down onto an oar – a blue tit, right beside my hand! I could hardly believe it, this beautiful little bird perched on my oar, cocking its head this way and that, trying to work out what I was.

I kept rowing, the same slow movement, the bird moving with the oar, unconcerned. My heart was thudding and I had to force myself to breathe.

'My God, will you look at that,' the fisherman whispered. He was leaning towards us, his rod forgotten.

For the minute or so the bird stayed on the oar, it felt as if time had stopped, as if the universe had paused in its business to give me this gift, this momentary encounter. Then it hopped onto the gunwale, looked around the boat and flew back to the trees on the shore.

On the boat, neither of us could find much to say. All the rest of the afternoon the fisherman sat quietly with his rod out, catching nothing. Every now and then he'd shake his head and I'd know he was thinking about it again.

'It was a while ago,' he said, 'but every time I think of it, I remember the wonder of that moment. The grace.'

She smiled and reached across the table and put her hand on his. He picked up her hand and kissed it, almost absently, then laid it down again, his eyes on hers except for the brief moment when he dipped his head to kiss.

'Thanks for telling me,' she said.

'You reminded me of it.'

'I did?'

'Whenever I look up and see you sitting beside me, it's like that moment.' He smiled then. 'I'm almost afraid to talk loud in case you fly away.'

'I've had enough of this! Enough of this shit!'

'It's just a bad patch,' he said reasonably. 'Listen, we can talk about it. Just calm down and we can talk about it.'

'Talk! Talk? That's all you ever bloody do, and it gets us nowhere!'

'Well, what do you want us to do then?'

'I don't give a toss what *you* do. But *I* want out of here.'

'No! It'll be ...'

'No, it won't be all right. It'll be more of the same: day after day of nothing very much, followed by days of complete shit, until nothing very much begins to seem like the best I'll ever have. And it's not good enough.'

'Maybe after ...'

'No. I've had it. I'm leaving. Now.'

'But where will you go?'

'I don't know and I don't care. Not here, that's all. I'll be back later in the week to pick up my stuff.'

She strode into the bedroom and he could hear opening drawers, the sound of a zip, tense silence while he imagined her forcing clothes into the bag, then another zip.

The bedroom door flew open and she came out, coat on, bag in hand, face determined and stony. She wrenched open the front door.

'Lewis,' he said. 'His name was Lewis.'

She stopped, hand on the doorknob, and turned to look at him. Her face was incredulous and angry.

'What?!'

'The ghillie who told me about the bird,' he said. 'I just remembered.'

She paused for a moment. 'That was long ago,' she said. She stepped out onto the landing and slammed the door behind her.

He stood still and listened to her footsteps all the way down the stairs. The street door opened and closed. If he moved to the window, he could watch her walking away. He stayed where he was, his fingers curled around his thumb.

# Unravelling

'I show you only the best!'

The shopkeeper beckoned us through to the back room. Jake and I sat down on a pile of rugs and looked around. The shopkeeper stuffed hashish into the bowl of a water pipe and passed it to me. I sucked hard on it until the smoke came through, then passed it to Jake. The merchant pulled carpet after carpet from a pile, letting us see each one before going on to the next. I reached for one of them and stroked the wool. It felt good.

'How much for this one?'

'You have dollars?'

'Some.'

'Only three hundred dollars.'

Jake laughed, coughing out a cloud of smoke. He turned over the corner of the carpet and shook his head. 'This is a shop carpet.'

The shopkeeper was outraged. 'No, effendi! This is antique!'

Jake held up the carpet, showing me the reverse side of the weave and some indecipherable marks in Persian script. 'Look,' he said, 'it is a new carpet. It's been on the shop floor for a few months to make it look older.'

The carpet was about seven feet by four, with an abstract pattern marked out by lines of deep green. Within these lines, oranges and yellows glowed. When the shopkeeper gave us a pipe to smoke, he was probably hoping for just this kind of effect.

I touched the orange, to see if I could feel the warmth of the colour. 'I like it anyway.'

'You see? This man, he knows a good carpet!'

Jake snorted and bent to the pipe again. The water gurgled as he drew in a good lungful of smoke.

'I'll give you fifty,' I said.

'Fifty! Is not possible!'

The baby crawled towards the carpet and you picked him up. 'That carpet can't stay there,' you said.

'Why not?'

'Well, look at it. Finlay can't crawl on that – it's not exactly clean, is it?'

I tried to look at the small carpet dispassionately. 'You're right. I'll Hoover it.'

'It needs more than that.' You grimaced. 'You don't know where it's been.'

I laughed. 'Oh yes I do. I certainly do!'

'Well, it needs cleaned.'

'All right, all right.'

It seemed a little disrespectful to put the carpet into the washing machine, but I could think of no other way to clean it thoroughly. Not knowing how the carpet would take it, I stuffed it in and turned the washing machine on: lowest temperature, gentlest wash. When it came out, I carried the heavy damp bundle to the washing line, hoping that it hadn't shrunk.

Jake was too stoned to travel with. I left him with some road-hippies in Kabul and headed back. It was a bad time of year to be travelling. The snow was still thick in Northern Turkey, and the bus was old and cold. Every few miles we passed the wreck of a bus or an articulated lorry. Walls of snow edged the road. The constant attrition of grit and slush had carved the snow into baroque sculptures, white towers edged with black residue from diesel exhaust. I drowsed, dreaming that these random snow-sculptures had a meaning and I could almost decipher them. Every now and then I woke, thinking – this is delirium brought on by hypothermia. The man sitting beside me looked like a Turkish bandit. He had a savage nose and a wild moustache. I sat close to the window, giving him as much space as I could.

At the next stop, I got the driver to open the luggage compartment and I untied the carpet from my rucksack. I climbed back onto the bus. Thirty or forty Turks watched me curiously – and me without a word of Turkish, apart from 'ekmek,' bread. When we started again, I laid the carpet on my legs to keep warm.

The bandit looked at me, then away. He probably carries a knife, I thought. I tucked the carpet snug. It was still six hours to Istanbul. My eyelids were beginning to droop when I caught the eye of the Turkish bandit. He scowled and nodded sharply. I turned away. He tapped me on the shoulder. I kept looking out of the window, desperately wondering what to do. The fierce Turk took my shoulder and shook it and I had to turn round to face him.

'What? What do you want?'

He scowled and nodded once more, then he jabbered something and poked my knee with his finger.

I held up my hands. 'Listen, man, I don't know what's wrong, but whatever it is, it's not my fault, right?'

He sighed, picked up my carpet and carefully draped it over both my lap and his.

'Oh!' I started laughing. 'Yes, okay. No problem.'

He patted my knee, patted his own. 'Okay?' he asked, his eyebrows raised.

'Yes, yes. Very okay.'

I sat there, grinning to myself. After a while I sensed movement from the Turkish bandit and he nudged me again. 'Ekmek?' He tore a chunk off his loaf and passed it to me.

I smiled and nodded and used the entirety of our shared vocabulary: 'Ekmek okay.'

When I got home from work, I saw it hanging there, blowing in the wind. The pattern was clear once again, almost like it had been when I first saw it in the shop: the curlicues and the almost-flower shapes, the lines that might be Arabic calligraphy or might just be decoration. The oranges and the yellows were bright – but not quite as bright as I remembered. The dark green lines had faded to a blue. It showed no signs of shrinkage. I was glad that it had been washed.

I unpegged it. It felt lighter. Was that possible? I held it up in the sunlight and pinpricks of light came through. It had become worn.

I folded it carefully, carried it to the house and replaced it in front of the fire. You came through then.

'The carpet's clean,' I said.

'Good.'

'It's a bit worn, but look at the colours. That orange there, that's what I liked, when I first saw it. It looked warm, friendly.' I laughed at myself. 'Friendly? Well, it did.'

'Cup of coffee? I'm just having one. Finlay's still asleep, thank God.'

'Yes, coffee, thanks.' I straightened the carpet before following her through to the kitchen.

I was hitching north through Spain. It was July, and very hot. I got a lift with four penniless French students. At nightfall, we pulled off the road. The ground was stony, with scattered bushes. The sky was clear and the night was warm. I rolled the carpet around me and slept on the ground.

Finally finding work, I needed a place to stay. I found a room in a shared house. It was a grim room. Bare boards for a floor, bare walls and a bare light bulb. The furniture was a shoogly bed with two thin blankets and two coarse sheets. I laid the carpet on the floor and I was home.

At a conference in Salzburg, we all stayed in a hostel run by nuns. It was a bit of a surprise, but it didn't seem to inhibit anyone, so I joined in the drinking and dancing until late at night.

Next morning, I felt awful. Not hungover, but shattered. I couldn't face the idea of travelling. The place was stirring, people heading for breakfast. I needed quiet. In an annexe, there was a meditation room – I'd seen the sign on the wall, in three languages. I slipped downstairs, left my rucksack in the corridor and entered the room. It had high windows and a blond wooden floor, and it was wonderfully quiet. I did a few simple exercises. Two other people came in and did likewise, silently. Then another person, and a few more. Soon there were a dozen of us, all silently stretching and bending.

Enter the Master. No question about that. Built like a tank, with a shaven head and an Oriental face. The silence became even more silent. He pulled a small bell from his robe and rang it. Everyone arranged themselves on the floor cross-legged. I sat down too. He frowned, pointed to the others, then back at me, saying something in German. I looked around. Everyone else had brought a mat.

I smiled and held up one finger. I slipped out of the door and returned with the carpet. I rolled it out and sat again. The Master grunted, rang his bell and began chanting strange syllables, not in German. We all closed our eyes. Afterwards I had breakfast and left, and I still have no idea who he was.

I pushed the last spoonful of mush towards Emily's face and she turned sideways. I wiped the food off her ear and let her out of the high chair. Finlay came screaming into the living room, arms spread, being a jet plane. He stopped beside Grace, who was building a city and had Lego all around her.

'There's been a crash landing,' he told her. 'Everyone has just been wiped out in a giant fireball!'

'Can you please go outside, if you're going to crash-land,' I said.

Emily was crawling over to the fireguard. I wiped the tray with her bib.

'It was a power dive. I had to wipe out an alien invasion.'

Emily was pulling herself upright, the wires of the fireguard squashing into her little plump fingers.

'Fine, but can't they invade the garden?'

Finlay was quiet for a moment while I folded the high chair. 'They're descended from cockroaches,' he said. 'They don't like the sunlight.'

'You're too clever by half. But no more screaming in the house.'

Emily saw Grace, playing with the Lego, head bent, long hair falling straight down. She loved Grace's hair. It was golden and shiny and her favourite thing in the world was to get one hand in among it and rub it against her own ear. She looked down at the carpet and her knees began to bend. Then she stood upright again and let go of the fireguard, lurching towards Grace.

'Jean,' I called, as loudly as I could without distracting Emily. 'Jean, she's walking!'

I heard your feet clattering down the stairs and the door opened. You stood there and I sat still, watching. Even Finlay was motionless for a moment. Emily took another step, caught her foot in the carpet and fell onto her knees among the Lego.

'That carpet has to go,' you said, while Emily was being cuddled and comforted.

'It's just a little frayed...'

'Yes. And it's dangerous. Emily fell today, but it could be Grace tomorrow, or anyone.'

I sighed. 'OK. I'll move it.' I folded it and took it upstairs. It wasn't really that bad, just a little looseness in the weave at one end. But it really ought to be out of the way, at least until Emily could walk properly. I went into our bedroom and laid it down at the foot of the bed and it was instantly at home.

'Look,' I said, later. 'Isn't that a good place for it?'

'Oh,' you said.

'It looks good there.'

'I suppose so.'

The Intercontinental Hotel, Amman. I was overwhelmed by the opulence of it, the subservient staff, the immense and wonderful buffet breakfast table.

Coming back after a day's work, the lobby was cool enough to make me shiver. I went to my room and sat there. The expenses didn't extend to visiting the Starlight Night Club up on the roof. There was nothing to do and underneath the excessive comfort, it was just another anonymous hotel. But this was my lodging for the next few weeks. I took the carpet from my luggage and laid it out on the soft flooring.

When I got home from work, the cleaners had carefully folded it and put it away on the slatted luggage rack in the wardrobe. I took it out again. Each day, they put it away. Each evening, I took it out again.

The only Jordanian I ever spoke to was my driver, Jamil. He thought I was beautiful. He said so. Then he winked and stroked my shoulder. I dissuaded him, forcefully, but we were still friends. He started teaching me Arabic words and phrases. It was something to do on the long drive out to the site. He taught me Muslim affirmations, and was delighted when I picked it up. He was half-laughing at me, I'm sure, but I joined in the game.

La illaha il allahu! We shouted the phrases in the car as we sped recklessly along the road. Alhamdulillah!

In the hotel, after eating, I took a penny whistle from my bags and tweetled to myself. I couldn't hold a tune, but there was no-one to hear – and the resonance of the room made it sound better. I put the whistle down and tried out the phrases Jamil had taught me. Alhamdulillah! Bismillah! They rang out in a very satisfying way.

In the morning, I always ran through a checklist before I left. Wallet in the pocket, plans in the shoulder bag, passport in the bag strung around my neck. All okay. I turned the door handle and quickly scanned the room. Hardly a sign of human habitation, except the untidy bed and, on the floor, the carpet – which would be neatly tidied away when I returned. Before I left the room, I called out loudly. La illaha il allahu!

It sounded great.

I turned from locking the door, and the cleaners were in the hall, a few yards away. They watched me intently. They must have heard me shouting in my room. I could feel myself blushing as I walked past them.

When I got back that evening, the carpet was where I had left it, though the rest of the room had been tidied.

When I got back from Amman, I needed a place to stay, and for the first time in my life, I didn't want to rent. I wanted something more permanent. When you came up to my flat for coffee, the first time, that carpet was on the floor, in front of the fireplace, where an electric fire stood on the tiled hearth. We turned off all the lights, but left the fire on, so that the room was warm and dim. The glow fell on you and me, and it fell on the carpet. There was nowhere to sit, nowhere to sleep, there was nothing else in the flat.

'This bedroom needs redecorated.'

'Does it?'

'Of course it does. Look at the handprints on the wall. The felt-tip pen. The... What is that?'

'Don't know.'

'Well, it was fine while the kids were young, but now it needs redone.'

'Mhm.'

'Blue? Or peach. What do you think?'

'Whatever you like.'

'No, tell me what you'd like.'

'Blue.'

'Not peach?'

'Blue.'

You redecorated it one weekend while I was away with the girls, climbing Arkle. We stayed in the bothy and came back late on Sunday. You must have been working non-stop. The bedroom was bright and fresh and new.

'Wow! What a job you've done. It looks great.'

You simpered theatrically. 'Oh it was nothing. Just a lick of paint, a new carpet and an inspired sense of style.'

I looked around. 'Where's the carpet?'

'On the floor, silly.'

'No, the little one, my carpet.'

'Oh, it really doesn't go with the peach. I put it in the utility room. It's a bit shabby. I hadn't realized how bad...'

'It's all right.'

You shrugged. 'I think it's about time we got rid of it.'

'Time we got rid of it?'

'Yes, you know. Time we replaced it.'

'We replaced it? We?'

'What do you mean?'

'*We* shan't replace it, because it's not *ours*. It's mine.'

Your lips tightened. 'It's frayed at the edges, it's threadbare and it's faded. It's time it was thrown out.'

You said it flat, in the tone of an ultimatum. My heart thudded loudly and my chest felt too tight to breathe. I couldn't think of anything to say, while you looked at me, and I didn't even know where to start. Because I could see that it was not an accident, this little argument. It was the latest move in a long campaign. You wanted rid of that carpet.

Half a lifetime ago, I bought a carpet in Kandahar. It warmed my legs and those of a Turkish bandit, it has given me shade in the heat. It has been a prayer rug and an exercise mat. It has been my blanket and my bed in railway stations, in buses, on ferries and on the hard ground. Wherever I was, I only had to lay it out and I knew that I was home. There have been times when it was all I owned, apart from my clothes. I didn't try to hang on to it, it just happened. One day, suddenly, it's twenty-five years later and the carpet is still here, and nothing else is still here.

But while the words filled my head, they wouldn't come out of my mouth. You can tell when someone is not ready to listen, you can tell when a mind is made up.

'This carpet has been with me for half my life,' I said. 'It's been to places you can't imagine.'

'A pity,' you said, 'that you didn't leave it in one of those places.'

With a leaden thump, an insight fell into place. You were jealous of my carpet. And the amazing thing was, you were right to feel jealous. I love that carpet, though I hadn't realized it until that moment.

As the words came out, I knew they were going to cause trouble. 'I've known that carpet longer than I've known you,' I said. 'It belongs here.'

What an odd way, I thought, for our life to fall apart.

# Girl

I am at the head of the jetty, fixing my boat.

She is standing at the roadside, her rucksack at her feet. Waiting.

I speak to her, of course – but she doesn't want to converse. I talk on for a while and she doesn't seem to mind, though she doesn't answer. When I fall silent, she looks around at the long bay and the hills, a few white houses and the hotel.

'I do not like this country,' she says.

It saddens me to hear it, but I just nod and gaze at the sea. Now that the tide has turned, the kelp along the jetty is streaming away from us, trying to follow the ebb.

She leans to read the blurred bus timetable on the post at the roadside. She has a pony tail, and the loose ends are blowing in the breeze. Her hair is brown, a rich brown, very like the colour of the kelp. I can see her cheek, the skin slightly freckled.

The boys come in from the salmon fishing, their thigh boots rolled down to their knees.

'Aye, boys,' I say, and nod at them. They look at the girl standing by her rucksack. She looks up the road to see if the bus is coming.

The boys, who are of course not boys at all, but men, both young and not so young, are looking forward to a drink in the bar. So they just wave as they cross the road. 'How's it going, Alec?' Then they go into the hotel and I turn away to look at the sea again.

The girl sighs and I wish to say something to make her feel better.

'Look,' I say, 'The gulls have found the herring.'

The blue sea has patches of grey where the breeze is moving across it. Above a blue patch there is a flurry of gulls, flecks of white hovering then dropping onto the water.

She looks without interest to where I am pointing.

A voice speaks behind me. 'I'll maybe take the boat out later.'

'Man! You gave me a fright. I thought you'd all gone in.'

He steps forward and stands beside me, so that we're standing there together.

'Well, Alec.'

'Well, Ally John.'

The girl looks up the road again, then turns to ask, 'Is the bus on time by custom?'

Now she can see Ally John and he can see her. I hesitate, long enough for Ally John to step in.

'It's late as often as not,' he says. He and the girl are looking at each other, and there is a smile between them. There is a flash of light on the hill, possibly from the windscreen of a bus, where the road comes round from Alligin. I see it, and perhaps Ally John sees it, but the girl doesn't see it.

'Will you take a drink with me,' he asks, 'while you're waiting?'

'But if the bus should come,' she says, 'I will be abandoned here.'

Ally John is not very used to women. He was a quiet boy, and he has been a quiet youth, excepting the few times when he has the drink in him. Then he goes wild and does the things that young men do, jumping off the bridge, swimming across the loch, driving too fast until he crashes his car.

So Ally John does not know what to do now. He knows the bus will be there in a minute or two. I can almost see them leaning towards one another, youth to youth, and it makes me feel both sad and happy, as the way is.

'I've been thinking about going up to Achnasheen later,' I say. 'I could give you a lift, if that would be of any use to you?'

She laughs. She doesn't know where Achnasheen is, but it gives her a chance to accept Ally John's invitation.

'Come on then,' says Ally John. 'Let me carry your bag.'

The bus goes past as they're settling into the table by the window. She doesn't even look.

The low afternoon light was in my eyes and I could only see her dark outline. I lifted my hand to block the sun. She reached out and took my hand, as she climbed into the boat. My heart lifted when her hand touched mine, thinking for a moment that I was young enough for it to mean something. Then she stepped over to her seat and blew a kiss to Ally John. He waved, then turned back to sorting nets with the other salmon fishers.

I started the engine and took the boat out until the marks lined up. 'This is the place for fish,' I said.

She fished at the bow and I at the stern, and the sun laid a golden path on the water as it went down. When the sun was gone, a piece of moon shone on us. I did not want to go in, though we were catching nothing at all. The girl was quiet in the bow, but she smiled to herself now and then, and looked at the hills growing dark around us.

'I like this place,' she said once, and then I was content. When the streetlights had come on in the village, I wound in my line and got the engine ready.

'Time to go in.'

She looked at me and smiled. 'Do we have to?'

'Will you be coming back, at all?' I thought I knew the way it was, but it's best to be sure.

'I don't like this country,' she said. 'It is cold.'

So I knew that she was going for good. I did not want to seem like an old gossip, but I thought I should ask, to be sure.

'Ally John?'

'He does not like me now. Perhaps I am not beautiful for him any more.'

'Surely it must be with Ally that the fault lies,' I said. 'You are like the land itself, standing up to look on itself. Your hair is like the seaweed, where the sun shines through the water; your neck is like the plover's egg hidden on the hillside.'

She looked up the road to see if the bus was coming, and I knew that I was too old for her to hear me. Or perhaps I did not speak. Perhaps I only said that I hoped she had a good trip.

'There will always be something of you left here,' I said. She looked bitter, and I knew she was remembering Ally. 'For it is myself that will be remembering you a long time.'

I knew she would not understand the Gaelic, but I was sad,

and that is the way I talk to myself when I am sad. It seems more homely, and closer to my heart.

When the bus came I lifted her rucksack for her and waited for the bus to go. She waved and I waved back, stiffly, without the thoughtless grace that young folk have when someone they love goes away.

# Calling to a Stranger

He was taken by surprise, no doubt about it. He had grown used to his life – and it was a fine and rewarding life with enough of a family and friends that he never had to be alone if he didn't want to be. Not well-off, but not exactly poor: there was enough slack to allow occasional luxuries – an outing to the cinema or an Indian meal when neither of the adults felt like cooking.

Or driving halfway down the country to an outdoor party in a wooded glen.

Of course, he had responsibilities, and he had to deal with them first. The garden gate needed fixed. An elderly parent needed visiting. He helped one of his daughters with her homework before he left. Then he slung his bag into the car and nervously drove off down the road.

Nervous? Yes, of course he was. He was going by himself. His wife had decided that it was not her kind of thing, though he was welcome to go. And after twenty years, he'd forgotten how to attend a party by himself.

Hillsides glowed in the late sunshine; every now and then the low sun dazzled him so that he had to slow the car on right-hand bends. It kept him alert. On a straight stretch of road he scrabbled the photocopied map out of the glove compartment to check the directions. The map had been hand-drawn and it was way out of scale so that the farm-track to the party site was drawn as wide as the A9. But the route was clear: turn left at the town, follow the signs for the glen, turn off at an old mill by the roadside

It was a good party. He danced for a while, he ate, he talked with a young woman who loved his accent, he talked with a man who'd lost his dog, he had a drink and he danced some more.

He wasn't a typical Scot. He didn't just stand in one spot and sway about. He moved from place to place, he enjoyed the music and it was obvious that he enjoyed it. He talked to

140

people while he danced and then he slipped away again, still dancing. Some people he knew and some he didn't, and they were all friendly. The scent of woodsmoke blew across the dance floor.

He marveled at himself, seeing how much he was enjoying the party. The music pounded, the people danced, and he was part of it. He was happy.

I don't want you to be misled on this point. He *was* happy. For a long time – hours it seemed – every part of him was filled with the night and the party and the music. Completely full. Then something popped into the fullness, where you'd scarcely think there was room for it. It was a thought or a realization, and it didn't have words. But if it did have words, it might have been something like – if I have so many friends and family that I need never be alone, why do I feel alone so often?

And he stopped there, on the dance floor and something poured into him. All the fullness was replaced with something that felt like a cry. It was without words, and it filled him until it overflowed and flooded out through the crowd and out into the night. It was beautiful and agonizing at the same time and he did not know what it was until it had subsided.

Then he found himself, in all that happy crowd, standing still, filled with the echoes of the feeling that had just passed through him.

That was yearning, he told himself in amazement, then shrank in embarrassment. He had been so open, so much a part of the dance that it seemed that everyone must have heard that silent cry, everyone must have felt that wave of anguish. He felt his cheeks burn, his heart thud. He slipped out of the courtyard and past the house, not meeting anyone's eyes. He followed the path down to the bonfire.

There's something about a fire. It encourages friendly chatter and long companionable silences. Music was coming from the courtyard by the house. Lanterns were lighting the path. Above, the night was dark and friendly.

He relaxed then, and found a space to sit on the logs that had been laid out as benches. He stared into the flames, letting himself melt into the heat, letting everything go. Drowsiness settled on him, and he thought he might find his car and have a sleep.

Then someone took him by the shoulders and turned him away from the fire.

'Look at the stars!'

He looked up and there was a woman, her face turned up to the dark sky. Beyond her face, the stars were blazing brightly. He watched them for a few seconds, then turned to the woman. She had moved away and was talking to someone else now, and all he could see of her was her hair, long and straight and blonde, hiding her face. Even so, he was sure that she was a stranger.

He shrugged, then stood and walked a few paces into the dark, to see the stars better.

When he came back, his place was taken. He glanced around and caught a glimpse of the woman, half-hidden behind someone else, so that all he could see was part of her profile – an eye and a cheekbone and her hair falling across her face. He walked around the fire, looking for a place to sit. He turned his head, and there she was again, half-visible between two other people. He found a seat, but the breeze blew smoke at him. He moved, then moved again. Every time he lifted his head, she was there; every time, her face was half-hidden by the fall of her hair, and now and then, she glanced at him, then away. He picked up a stick and pushed it into the fire, shielding his face from the heat, trying to get the stick right into the heart. He pulled back at last and lifted his head – and there she was, across the fire, half-visible through the flames. Everywhere he turned, she was there.

'Bugger this,' he muttered. He kept his head down for a few minutes, then quietly slipped off his seat and headed back up the path.

Not three yards in front of him was the woman, walking towards the house.

He paused for half a step, then continued. She went into the house and, with a sense of relief, he went by, to the dance floor.

Time to back out a bit. We're not watching an idiot here. He's well aware of the effects of party atmosphere and party stimulants. He hasn't been sticking to alcohol, we can be sure of that. It's that kind of party. I can see him afloat in the whirlpool of excitement and illusion that is a party. And right about now, I see him putting out his storm-anchor. He has found a couple of friends and they have gone inside – they are drinking mugs of tea in the kitchen. The intensity of the moment, the compelling quality, is passing. A few minutes of gathering himself and all will be well.

He laughs with his friends, lifts his mug to his lips and lets his eyes close – and there she is, in his mind's eye, glancing at him over someone's shoulder, her hair falling across her face.

At this point, he grits his teeth and admits to himself that there is something here that needs to be dealt with. He is not happy about it – indeed he feels angry about being forced into this situation. But he has finally realized that unless he does something, he's not going to enjoy the party.

She'll be at the fire. He knows this. He just knows. So he walks down towards the fire – and turns back. He simply doesn't know what to do. He has never learnt a strategy for speaking to unknown women who won't leave his mind. Anyone else at the party, *anyone* else, he could just go up and say, 'Hi, how's it going? Great party, isn't it?' But that's not good enough for her. There's something going on and he needs to get to the bottom of it.

He manages to force himself down the path to the fire, and then he looks around for her. He is not surprised to find that he is standing right beside her and she is talking to her friends.

He walks up and down in the twilight between the fire and the dark, waiting for a suitable moment to speak to her – but she just sits there, her back to him, talking to her friends. There is a space on a log a few places round. He goes over there and sits, hoping for some social miracle to give him the chance to speak.

But nothing happens except that every now and then she glances at him, then back to whoever she's speaking to, her face mostly hidden by the fall of her hair.

Then he knows what he has to do. He stands up, walks in among her group and speaks to her.

'Could I have a word with you?' He gestures away from the fire. 'Just for a minute?'

'Sure.'

He turns and walks out into the twilight, she following. Then he turns and, for the first time, sees her entire face.

If there was any doubt about it, it is gone now. She is a complete stranger.

'I need to know who you are,' he says baldly, and she tells him. Just like that, no hesitation, with no sign of misgiving, as if this was just what she'd been waiting for.

He's hardly listening. He even has to interrupt her to get her to repeat her name. Then she stops.

'How about you?' she asks.

He hadn't even thought beyond the moment when he asked to speak to her. He bumbles out his reply, half-expecting her to make her excuses and leave – but she doesn't. He talks, then she talks – then he talks again and five minutes later they are sitting together by the fire discussing books. He has barely a clue what they are talking about, but he knows that as long as she's talking or he's talking, he can keep looking at her. He needs to watch her, needs to watch for some clue about who she is and why she won't leave his mind.

Something she says sticks in his head. There is a break in the conversation. He listens to what she has just said: 'I came here with my boyfriend.'

'Oh?'

'That's him over there.' She waves to a man across the fire. He is watching them.

There is a silence, then she speaks again.

'You were talking about your favourite book.'

'Ah. Yes. Well, at the moment, it's the one I just finished reading. Holes, by Louis Sachar. Lovely book. It may be a children's book, though it's not marketed as one. But my daughter read it after me.'

'Your daughter? How old is she?'

'She's twelve – and the other one's nine.' He smiled. 'They

144

both love reading.'

She was looking straight at him as she said, 'And you're still with their mother?'

'Ah ... Yes.' And for the first time in ten minutes he looked away from her, down at the ground. Then he looked her in the face again. 'Yes, I am,' he said with surety, because whatever was going on here, marriage and boyfriends had little to do with it.

She nodded and kept her eyes on his. Oddly, her face had seemed anonymous until then. Just the face of a woman. Now he realized that her eyes were gray and that she was lovely.

'Oh dear,' he said.

And it never occurred to him that he might never see her again. Not until two days later, when he was tidying his car. He found the hand-drawn map and crumpled it up to throw it away. Then he stopped. If he saw her again, the map was unimportant – but if he didn't, that map was the only sign he had that the party had happened, that something had passed between two people by the fire.

So he didn't keep it; but he couldn't bear to throw it away either. The crumpled map still lies on the floor of his car. He will throw it out when he loses hope or when she comes back into his life. Until then, it is a sad object on the floor of his car, which, personally, I can hardly bear seeing.

I think he should have thrown it out.

# Fiction from Two Ravens Press

## Highland Views
### David Ross

Military jets exercise over Loch Eye as a seer struggles to remember his vision; the honeymoon is over for workers down at the Nigg yard, and an English incomer leads the fight for independence both for Scotland and for herself... This début collection of stories provides an original perspective on the Highlands, subtly addressing the unique combination of old and new influences that operate today.

'I'm a big fan. A fine organic collection that advances a viewpoint, culture and history quite other than the urban central belt that still lopsidedly dominates recent Scottish literature.' **Andrew Greig**

'A view of the Highlands with a strong element of political and social comment. Ross explores these concerns in convincingly human terms through the lives of his characters.' **Brian McCabe**

'...An authentic and unsentimental aspect on Highland life. The characters are real, the prose is lyrical and the stories compelling.'
**The Scots Magazine**

£7.99. ISBN 978-1-906120-05-4. Published April 2007.


## Types of Everlasting Rest
### Clio Gray

From Italy and Russia in the time of Napoleon to the fate of Boy Scouts in Czechoslovakia during the Second World War, Clio Gray's short stories are filled with intrigue, conspiracy and murder. Laden with sumptuous detail, each story leads the reader directly into the compelling and sometimes bizarre inner worlds of her fascinating characters.

'Clio Gray is a master of atmosphere and sensuousness. She combines historical realism with the bizarre, whimsy with the macabre. Reading her is like being at a sumptuous feast in a palace, just before it is stormed.' **Alan Bissett**

'...powerful stuff ... worth savouring. Clio Gray is an uncommonly interesting writer. One wonders, expectantly, what she will do next.'
**Allan Massie, The Scotsman**

'... fresh, original, beautifully written... a highly impressive collection.'
**Lesley McDowell, Scottish Review of Books**

£8.99. ISBN 978-1-906120-04-7. Published July 2007.

# Riptide: New Writing from the Highlands & Islands
## Sharon Blackie & David Knowles (Eds)

This diverse collection of new fiction and poetry from the Highlands & Islands showcases the work of established writers and new names to watch.

**Contributors:**

Pam Beasant, Sharon Blackie, Robert Davidson, Angus Dunn, Eva Faber, Alison Flett, Yvonne Gray, John Glenday, Clio Gray, Andrew Greig, Nicky Guthrie, Mandy Haggith, Morag Henderson, Elyse Jamieson, Laureen Johnson, David Knowles, Morag MacInnes, Anne Macleod, Kevin MacNeil, Daibhidh Martin, John McGill, Donald Murray, Alison Napier, Pauline Prior-Pitt, Joanna Ramsey, Cynthia Rogerson, David Ross, Mark Ryan Smith, and Peter Urpeth.

'...*a force of creation, the kind of irresistible tide into which we should dip.*' *The Scotsman*

£8.99. ISBN 978-1-906120-02-3. Published April 2007.

# The Long Delirious Burning Blue
## Sharon Blackie

Cat Munro's safe, carefully-controlled world as a corporate lawyer in Phoenix is disintegrating, and she is diagnosed with panic disorder just before her fortieth birthday. In a last-ditch attempt to regain control of her life, she faces up to her greatest fear of all: she decides to learn to fly. As she struggles to let go of old memories and the anxieties that have always held her back, Cat faces a choice: should she try to piece her old life back together again, or should she give in to the increasingly urgent compulsion to throw it all away?

Several thousand miles away in Scotland, Cat's mother Laura faces retirement and a growing sense of failure and futility. Alone for the first time in her life, she is forced to face the memories of her violent and abusive marriage, the alcoholism that followed, and her resulting fragile relationship with Cat. But then she joins the local storytelling circle. And as she becomes attuned to the mythical, watery landscape around her, she begins to reconstruct the story of her own life...

From the excoriating heat of the Arizona desert to the misty flow of a north-west Highland sea-loch, Sharon Blackie's first novel presents us with landscape in all its transformative power. An honest and moving exploration of the complexities of mother-daughter relationships, *The Long Delirious Burning Blue* is above all a story of courage, endurance and redemption.

'*An inspirational literary début; empathetic and mature. Sharon Blackie vividly conveys the protagonist's struggle to overcome her fear of flight to crack open the limitations imposed on her, not just by others but by the memory of others.*' **Margaret Graham**

'Sharon Blackie writes with a real sense of truth and emotional depth about relationships between individuals, and between individuals and their environment. Her characters are figures in a landscape brought vividly, vibrantly to life.' *Nicholas Royle*

£8.99. ISBN 978-1-906120-17-7. Published February 2008.

# Auschwitz
## Angela Morgan Cutler

Auschwitz: a place where millions were killed and which thousands now visit each year. A mass grave – and a tourist destination. The focus of this work of autobiographical fiction is on the sightseers – the curious that are drawn to visit. It is a book that questions our need to look: what is there to uncover, other than the difficulty of peering into such a place and into a subject that has been obsessively documented, yet can never really be understood? How to write about Auschwitz in the twenty-first century, in a time when the last generation of survivors is soon to be lost?

This is also a book that searches for a personal story. It opens on a local bus that takes Angela, her husband En (whose mother survived the holocaust where most of her family did not) and their two sons to Auschwitz sixty years after the holocaust, and ends in a pine forest outside Minsk where En's grandparents were shot in May 1942.

The backbone of *Auschwitz* is a series of e-mails between the author and acclaimed Franco-American writer Raymond Federman. This beautiful, powerful and innovative work experiments with new forms – correspondence, reflections, dreams, a travelogue – that mirror the fragmentary legacy of the holocaust itself and that, at the same time, capture its contradictions – and sometimes its absurdity.

'*Auschwitz stands like a tombstone for our civilisation. Angela Morgan Cutler has brilliantly infiltrated the borders of this landscape of desolation. Somehow she has found a voice that reflects the enormity of the horrors perpetuated there without being stifled by them. Unsentimental and richly worked ... the words are more than mere messengers of thoughts and feelings---they glow with a life of their own ... the whole package quite inimitable: the rarest quality in literature.' Henry Woolf*

£9.99. ISBN 978-1-906120-18-4. Published February 2008.

# The Last Bear
## Mandy Haggith

A haunting and compelling novel set one thousand years ago in the remote northwest Highlands of Scotland, *The Last Bear* recounts a tale of ecological and spiritual crisis from the viewpoint of one extraordinary woman.

Taking the story of the extinction of the brown bear as its focal point, a story of love, jealousy, family and faith unfolds as Brigid, the last in a long line of medicine women, tries to live out her life in a time of upheaval without losing her cultural roots. Her personal struggle is set against a transforming world, as powerful Viking families clash with Celts and old pagan beliefs are challenged by Christian faith, changes that reach even into the timeless depths of the forest.

Haggith weaves evocative descriptions of the natural world into a narrative that binds the characters ever more tightly into intrigue. Who killed the last bear in Scotland, and with what consequences?

'The Last Bear *is as much poem as prose, a lament for the last bear in Scotland, and the human ways of life that died with her. With the imposition of an alien religion the old harmonies are disrupted; the last bear is the final sacrifice of the old order.* The Last Bear *focuses on a pivotal historical moment, yet the results echo on down the centuries: the pain and loss of the last bear is, in fact, our own.'*
Margaret Elphinstone

£8.99. ISBN 978-1-906120-16-0. Published March 2008.

# One True Void
## Dexter Petley

They still called him Pisspot, the local scrubbers and all his ex-classmates, as they whizzed around the village on their Motobecanes. They didn't understand why he wasn't hanging about up the chip shop with them any more, or phlobbing cheese and onion curd outside the public bar of The Royal Oak and playing inside left for the second team. But it was 1973 and Henry Chambers, aged 17, was motivated to achieve greatness. He'd just found out that if he wanted to be a poet he had to have both a vision of himself and a Pre-Raphaelite girlfriend. But that was impossible in the dead winter village of Hawkhurst. And the Claires and Virginias of West Kent College, Tunbridge Wells already had the Jameses and Jollyons as their social equals. Not Henry, the quiet poet with the tumbleweed bumfluff and cotted hair. No: for Henry, the future was bleak. There was no point and no vision. But just as Henry was putting the black edges round his own stationery and plotting to murder his baggots, he visited an 'old lady' on his Thursday afternoon community service. The house was called Plato Villa and Maxine Pollenfex – not exactly the old lady he was expecting – was going to change Henry's life, and everyone else's, forever.

'Petley's style is like acid on a plate, biting into whatever it sees and leaving extraordinary linguistic marks." Derek Beaven
'Izaac Walton with attitude and Mogadon.' Tibor Fischer

£8.99. ISBN 978-1-906120-13-9. Published January 2008.

# Also by Two Ravens Press

Love Letters from my Death-bed: by Cynthia Rogerson
£8.99. ISBN 978-1-906120-00-9. Published April 2007

Nightingale: by Peter Dorward
£9.99. ISBN 978-1-906120-09-2. Published September 2007

Parties: by Tom Lappin
£9.99. ISBN 978-1-906120-11-5. Published October 2007

Prince Rupert's Teardrop: by Lisa Glass
£9.99. ISBN 978-1-906120-15-3. Published November 2007

The Most Glorified Strip of Bunting: by John McGill
£9.99. ISBN 978-1-906120-12-2. Published November 2007

Double or Nothing: a by Raymond Federman
£9.99. ISBN 978-1-906120-20-7. Published March 2008

The Falconer: by Alice Thompson
£8.99. ISBN 978-1-906120-23-8. Published April 2008

# Poetry from Two Ravens Press

The Atlantic Forest: by George Gunn
£8.99. ISBN 978-1-906120-26-9. Published April 2008

In the Hanging Valley: by Yvonne Gray
£8.99. ISBN 978-1-906120-19-1. Published March 2008

Running with a Snow Leopard: by Pamela Beasant
£8.99. ISBN 978-1-906120-14-6. Published January 2008

In a Room Darkened: by Kevin Williamson
£8.99. ISBN 978-1-906120-07-8. Published October 2007

Castings: by Mandy Haggith
£8.99. ISBN 978-1-906120-01-6. Published February 2007

The Zig Zag Woman: by Maggie Sawkins
£8.99. ISBN 978-1-906120-08-5. Published September 2007

Leaving the Nest: by Dorothy Baird
£8.99. ISBN 978-1-906120-06-1. Published July 2007

---

For more information on these and other titles, and for extracts and author interviews, see our website.

Titles are available direct from the publisher at
**www.tworavenspress.com**
or from any good bookshop.